X's for Eyes

Laird Barron

Bizarro Pulp Press
an imprint of JournalStone Publishing

Bizarro Pulp Press books may be ordered through booksellers or by contacting:

Bizarro Pulp Press, a JournalStone imprint
    www.BizarroPulpPress.com

    ISBN: 978-1-942712-82-4

Printed in the United States of America
JournalStone rev. date: November 4, 2015

    Cover Art: Matthew Revert
        www.matthewrevert.com
    Interior Formatting: Lori Michelle
        www.theauthorsalley.com

Praise for X's for Eyes

"[X's for Eyes is] so ripe with cosmic horror allusion and riffs that it qualifies as post-modern, but so charged with narrative drive that one can only hold on for dear life and hope to escape with their mind intact."
—Jeremy Robert Johnson,
author of *Skullcrack City*

"This has the narrative velocity of the best thirties pulp, the grim countenance and surly demeanor of the deadliest noir, and a premise the X-Files would wish for."
—Stephen Graham Jones,
author of *After the People Lights Have Gone Off*

Part I: We Smoke the Northern Lights

The White Devil

The boy awakened in the night, although he had cultivated sufficient wariness to not move a muscle beneath the leopard- and yak-hide blankets. He scanned the dim sleeping cell without turning his head. A torch sizzled in its sconce high in the corner. Hoarfrost rimed the threshold of the doorway. Wind tore at the shuttered window as snow seeped in and dusted the sill.

A stranger sat at the foot of the bed. Killing cold did not appear to discomfort him. He wore a Brooks Brothers suit with a red carnation pinned to the left breast pocket. His short black hair gleamed like polished metal. Some might have considered him queerly handsome or supremely repellant, depending. He said, "My name is Tom. Hello, son." Blandly unctuous, his skin and eyes and voice were odd. A plastic figurine, animated and life-sized, might have looked and sounded as Tom did. "Sifu has terrorized you well. Your problem is the same problem inherent to all primates, which is, you are a primate."

"Are you a friend of Sifu?" The boy was afraid. Ruthless discipline disguised his fear. He pretended to be unaffected by the presence of a fellow westerner decked out for a garden party. Only assassin monks and child students were permitted inside the temple, for it was built atop a remote peak of the inner Himalayas, hundreds of miles from civilization and its devils, white and otherwise.

"I'm Tom. Sifu Kung Fan is among the vilest, evilest wretches who has ever walked this planet. Of course he is a dear friend."

"Tom *who*, if you please?"

"Tom Mandibole."

"Good to meet you, Mr. Mandibole. What brings you to these parts?"

"I was once an anthropologist in service of a sultan. My master is bedridden, so to speak. He seeks diversion in the momentous and insignificant alike. Sadly, the Sultan marooned me here on this lee

1

shore. Like him, I take my pleasures, great and small, as the opportunity arises."

"I am sure you're a valuable servant. There must have been a misunderstanding."

"No, my boy. He stranded me because it amuses him to do so. The universe and its design is often one of arbitrary horror. Let none of this disturb you overmuch. You won't remember our conversation."

The boy considered his options, and decided to say nothing.

Tom Mandibole smiled and his mouth articulated stiffly. "I noticed your light as I walked by. A flame in the darkness is alluring."

"This seems far from beaten paths."

"I am abroad in the night with my servants. We come to smoke the northern lights, to rape the Wendigo, to melt igloos with streams of hot, bloody piss. To see and see."

"Oh. You're a bit east."

"As I said, I was walking past on my way to another place. Much colder, much darker, this other place. Although, I have seen colder and darker yet."

"The North Pole is swell. I've snowshoed the Kuskokwim Delta."

"Would you care to guess what I am, son?"

The boy shook his head.

Tom Mandibole's mouth contracted and he spoke without moving his lips. "I am the bane of your existence and I am going to tell you something. You will not remember, but it will embed itself like a dreadful seed in your young, impressionable mind. Now listen carefully." He uttered a few words, then slowly lowered himself into a Cossack dancer's squat. The stranger melted into the pool of red-tinged shadows that spread across the floor.

The boy shivered. Under the hides, he gripped the hilt of his kukri that, according to Sifu Kung Fan, had claimed the heads of two-score men, and stared at the ceiling until his eyelids grew heavy. He slept, and in the morning, as Tom Mandibole promised, remembered nothing of the visit.

Rendezvous at Woolfolk Bluff

The Tooms brothers returned home to the Mid-Hudson Valley in June of 1956 after another grueling winter at the Mountain Leopard Temple. A winter of calisthenics undertaken near, and sometimes over, bottomless chasms; instruction in advanced poisoning methods that included being poisoned; pillow talk, and master-level subterfuge occasionally incorporating assassination attempts upon students. Joyously free from the Himalayas for summer vacation, Macbeth and Drederick resolved to relish their R&R to the fullest.

The brothers dressed in casual suits, jackets, and ties, and hopped into Dad's cherry 1939 Chrysler fliptop for a cruise. Mac had heisted one and a half bottles of Glenrothes 18 from the pantry. Dred swiped a carton of Old Gold and Dad's third or fourth favorite deer hunting rifle. Berrien Lochinvar, the grizzled Legionnaire and lately butler, didn't bother to ask why or where. He waved forlornly from the mansion steps as the boys roared down the private drive and into a pink and gold MGM sunset. There might or might not be hell to pay later, depending upon the mood of Mr. and Mrs. Tooms when they returned from vacationing in Monaco. It was no coincidence the elder Toomses' vacation overlapped the boys' own.

The lads made a whistle-stop in Phoenicia to snag a couple of working girls at Greasy Dick's soda shop—Betsy & Vera. The girls' dates were raw-boned farmhands in the mood to blow their paychecks. Mac scoffed as he waved a fistful of Grants. The men riled at this most unwelcome intrusion by wet-behind-the-ears fancy pants brats. Dred showed them the rifle. The farmhands blustered and puffed their chests. He blasted out Dick's neon shingle. The men cooled it.

3

Mac goosed the Chrysler and drank from a bottle all the way to Woolfolk Bluff. Liquor didn't have much effect on his capabilities. It only made him more determined. He got them there in one piece and they paired off and shagged. Prior, during, and after, the foursome smoked a hell of a lot of the Old Gold and drank up all the booze.

"Jeezum crow." Blonde Betsy fastened her skirt. "How old are you, kid?" She squinted at Dred as if apprehending him for the first time. "Say, are you even twelve?"

"And a half." Dred reposed in the altogether, watching smoke from his mouth bump against the ceiling of stars. He was of average height, sturdy, with thicker, curlier hair than his brother. "Mac is fourteen."

"And a half," Mac said. A bit taller than Dred, slightly more kempt, and much denser and stronger than he appeared at first glance. He pointed the rifle at Orion's Belt and squeezed off a round. Missed, or too early to tell. "Is this buyer's remorse, ladies?"

"Yep, we're going to hell for sure," said Vera, the brunette.

"Oh, you were hellbound way before you met us," Dred said. "And for lots worse I'd wager. Those farm boys all have the syphilis."

"Fleas too." Betsy scratched at herself.

Vera said to Mac, "How come you kids got a funny Limey way a talkin'? Shagging? Who says shagging?"

Betsy said to Dred, "Yeah! And how come your accents keep changin'?"

"Our mother is Egyptian," Mac said. "She was educated at Oxford. I suppose her accent rubbed off."

"Your mama is a colored girl?" Vera raised her eyebrows.

"Mother is Mother." Mac said it cold and sober.

A meteor streaked across the sky. And another. The third object described a fiery red arc through the lower heavens and crashed down across the valley behind a ridge. *BOOOM!* The granddaddy of all thunderbolts thrummed in the earth. A reddish flash lit up the horizon. Trees shook in the grip of a concussion. To their credit, neither of the working girls screamed, although they clung to one another, perfect little mouths O-d in fear.

Dred tipped a salute at Mac. "Nice shootin', Tex."

Mac checked his watch. "Saved by the meteorite."

The boys dressed in a hurry. Mac tossed Vera the keys and told her to leave the car at Nelson's Garage in Phoenicia. He scratched their current coordinates on a paper scrap and gave her a number and instructions to buzz his dear pal, Arthur Navarro. Promised her fifty bucks if she came through. As the ladies of the night roared off in the Chrysler, Dred said, "Reckless trusting those girls with that much power, brother. Dad loves that car. I was conceived in the backseat."

Mac removed his glasses to wipe them. His eyes were red and watery. He shrugged and started walking.

"Hey! How did ya know?" Dred called.

"Arthur told me to hang around the bluff tonight," Mac said, as he disappeared over the rim. "We better make tracks. Fireworks like these, somebody will be on the way."

"Who will be on the way? The Army? The heat? Granddad?"

"Pick one and it isn't anybody we want to see."

Dred waved his arms in frustration. "I thought we'd driven all the way out here for a nice relaxing Friday night of debauchery. Meanwhile, you were hiding an ulterior motive up your sleeve." No response was forthcoming. He sighed and went after his big brother.

You're No Doc Savage!

The descent required a bit of free-climbing, and the boys were still half-crocked. Luckily, in addition to mandatory climbing lessons at Mountain Leopard Temple, they'd vacationed in the Swiss Alps every year since being weaned from their nursemaid's teat and were, as a consequence, expert mountaineers. The boys made it down with style after some minor scrapes due to poor light, and double-timed across a grassy field and up the far ridge.

"Mac, are we having an adventure? Is someone going to shoot at me? Am I going to be kidnapped again? Locked in a trunk and dropped into the sea? Experimented on with growth hormones? Chased by a lunatic in a mechanical werewolf getup? It sure feels like we're having an adventure."

"Yep, we're having an adventure," Mac said.

Amid a stand of pine and sycamore, some branches yet smoldering with licks of greenish flame, lay a shallow, smoke-filled depression. A metallic plate shone at the center of the crater—the outer curve of a partially buried space object.

"Well, that's sure as heck not a weather balloon," Dred said. "Since NACA is three years south of launching anything besides planes and rockets into low Earth orbit, the only question is, whose satellite? Ours or theirs?"

"It's not a satellite either."

"Ya don't say. Wait a—Holy Toledo! Is it alien? I'm gonna win a Nobel!"

"The Nobel doesn't award a prize for Acute Idiocy. Little green men don't exist, sorry to disappoint."

"The book ain't closed on extraterrestrial life."

"Say *ain't* again and I'll smack your mouth. It's *ours*, Dred. Sword Enterprises is way past satellites. You'd know this if you ever bothered to read an R&D report."

"Sorry, I'm busy crafting my body into the ultimate fighting and fornicating machine. NACA would love the scoop about Nancy is what I do know."

"Trust that a select government subcommittee is well aware. Who do you think coughs up a third of our research capital? When Granddad says foreign investors, he means a farm in Langley." Mac lighted a cigarette and braced his boot upon a rock. Red-lit smoke boiled in his glasses. "Our X-R program developed a long-range probe in '52. NCY-93. You're looking at Nancy, kid. Experimental phase, last I heard."

"Apparently, Granddad got her working." Granddad was better known by the world as Danzig Tooms, patriarch of the Eastern Toomses, and the reclusive industrialist who owned majority shares of multinational conglomerate, Sword Enterprises. He also directed R&D for space technologies.

"Hmm. My compass is dizzy."

"Mine too." Dred's mini-compass attached to his Swiss Army knife via a keychain. The needle revolved crazily. "Peculiar, eh? I'd expect it to point at the metal, if anywhere. Chunk this big has to be a false magnetic north."

"Yes. Peculiar." Mac laid two fingers against his own wrist and waited. "Elevated pulse. Hairs are standing on end. Possible auditory hallucinations—could be my brother's yammering. The object is generating a powerful electromagnetic field. Let's hope it's non-ionizing."

"Hallucinations? I'm not getting hallucinations. At least, I hope not. Maybe I am. Did ya hear somethin'? Pine needles are exploding. Seems normal, though. I mean, the trees are on fire, right?"

"I doubt you'd be able to tell the difference after that much scotch. C'mon, the breeze is shifting. Don't fancy a dose of radiation before breakfast."

They moved upwind of the wreckage and sheltered beneath an overhang of dead pine roots. Dred didn't pester his brother with questions about the probe or Sword Enterprises' top secret space program, referred to by insiders as Extraterrestrial Reconnaissance, or X-R. Mac refused to speak when he didn't want to, and, at the moment, his pinched lips and narrowed eyes indicated he surely didn't want to. Big brother wore that expression when struggling with angles, calculations, and worry. Nobody worried more intensely than Mac, except for Dad, possibly. Dred smoked and tried to figure the dimensions of the probe based on the length of the crash path and how much of the vehicle was exposed.

Eventually, Arthur "Milo" Navarro came along and rescued them from a fatal case of contemplating their navels. The Navarros weren't wealthy like the Toomses; Arthur's father, Luis, chaired the Engineering Corp of Sword Enterprises, and so were imbued with a significant measure of means and privilege, nonetheless. Arthur had graduated Graves College with honors. He intended to take a year away from his studies, travel Europe, and intern with the fellows at the Norwegian Academy of Science before plowing forward with his doctorate. His eighteenth birthday landed in August and the Tooms brothers promised him a shindig prior to the commencement of his overseas adventures.

Mac summoned him whenever he needed a big brain, or godly muscle. Arthur could easily have been the brightest kid in New York State. Few outside his circle of friends and associates were the wiser—he resembled a Sherman tank in his customary uniform of Carhartt dungarees (shirtless), and engineer boots. Low-browed, thick of jaw and neck, and grimly reticent, he played the part of a lug to perfection. Few ever got close enough to realize they'd crossed paths with a boy genius rather than a simple bruiser. Slow to anger, the surest way to kindle his ire was to yell, "You're no Doc Savage!" He'd collected every magazine and every comic, and recorded every radio show featuring the pulp hero. He'd even attempted to concoct a bronzing solution. Nobody with an iota of common sense mentioned the fiasco.

"Hail the crash site! A goodtime gal reported a pair of ne'er-do-wells in need of assistance." Arthur lumbered into the clearing. He was attended by two of his five younger brothers, Ronaldo and Gerard, and their manservant Kasper, an allegedly reformed Waffen-SS commando. The party members wore reflective hazmat suits and carried toolboxes. Arthur unpacked a Geiger-counter and performed a laborious circuit of the immediate vicinity. He removed his helmet and examined the exposed patch of hull. "We're clean." He gave orders to his companions. Kasper and the two boys started in with picks and steadily peeled away dirt to expose a broader plane of smooth, scorched metal.

Mac and Dred climbed down to join the fun.

"What do you think?" Mac asked. A relatively tall and sturdy young man, he was a peewee juxtaposed against Arthur Navarro.

"I think we need to be gone before trouble arrives," Arthur said.

Dred sighed in exasperation. "For Pete's sake, who are we expecting?"

"Maybe the Army," Mac said.

"I thought ya didn't know!"

"I don't. I'm making an educated guess."

"Not sure it's the military. Not sure of a blessed thing, honestly." Arthur popped the lid on a toolbox. He selected an industrial-sized hand drill. "I monitored the channels all night. The probe is designed to evade radar detection. Didn't hear a peep from the Army or the Air Force, which means the stealth system functioned like a champ. There's action, though. Twenty minutes ago, Ronaldo caught chatter on the emergency band."

He nodded at his sibling who smiled gamely through streams of sweat. "I thought Labrador had twigged to the deal, at first. The boys at Zircon have stolen loads of our tech and brain-drained enough of our researchers, seems a fair bet they've got the codes to track this pretty baby." He finished locking down a drill bit the length of his arm and squeezed the trigger. The motor shrieked. "Zircon hadn't the foggiest. The installation Ron eavesdropped on didn't spot the probe—Zircon intercepted a backchannel message from someone who did. Complete unknowns. A rival corporation, the CIA, hillbillies with a ham radio, anybody's guess."

"Swell," Mac said. He checked the bolt on the deer rifle. "What about my grandfather? Surely X-R is on top of this?"

"Our side isn't searching for Nancy. Two reasons. One, she's supposed to splash down in the Atlantic—that's the game plan, anyhow. Two, launch isn't scheduled until the 11th of June."

"Hey, hold the phone!" Dred said. "That's next week! Which means the probe launched in secret and earlier. Wait, wait—unless we're talking about multiple probes. My skull is aching."

"Nancy hasn't launched. Sword Enterprises possesses more resources than God, but even we can't afford multiple experimental space rockets this sophisticated."

"Fine. Then this is impossible."

"Absolutely. Step back, friend." Arthur snugged his welding goggles. He drilled through a series of rivets, paused to change the bit, and removed the bolts. A small plate came free, exposing a circuit board and toggles. He flipped the toggles in varying orders until an alarm chimed deep within the probe and an oval section of the hull a hand-span wide rolled back. From a maze of wires, Arthur drew forth a pair of slender trapezoidal tubes, each roughly a yard in length and constructed of crystal shot through with black whorls and lightning bolts.

Kasper swaddled the tubes in fireproof blankets. Dawn glinted among the gaps in the branches, a cool reddish glare that disquieted Mac for reasons he couldn't put his finger on.

"High time to make tracks," he said as the last of the equipment was stowed.

"Yeah, let's am-scray," Dred said. "I've got the heebie-jeebies."

Big Black

The company hustled a quarter mile to where a two-ton canvas-backed farm truck awaited. Everybody piled in. Kasper drove through underbrush and between copses of paper birch, pine, and mulberry, until he hit a dirt road that wound along the valley floor and eventually merged with the highway. By consensus they decided to transport their prize to Mac and Dred's house. Nowhere more secure except for corporate headquarters, and HQ was a last resort due to the fact Dr. Bole and chief of security Nail would demand an explanation.

Kasper circled past Rosendale and took a secret access road that tunneled through Shawangunk Ridge and emerged at a huge old barn (the boys' clubhouse) on the edge of the Tooms manor's back forty. The interior of the barn contained a workshop, lab, a computer, and basement storage. An antenna array poked through the roof. Reinforced with battleship armor plates and powered courtesy of a thirty kilowatt diesel generator sealed inside a soundproof boiler compartment, the barn seemed a likely command post of opportunity.

"Fellows, I don't understand any of this," Dred said.

"You're three sheets to the wind," Mac said.

"So are you, brother."

"None of us have a bead on the details," Arthur said. He glanced at Mac. "Did you notice how slender the crystals are? Those are fabricated in a geovault. Specially engineered and grown. I've seen the tubes as they're inserted into the mainframe. The ones we extracted were mature when the technicians embedded them in Nancy. Which means they should be heavier, fuller. Then there's the internal composition. The discoloration indicates data saturation."

"I saw. It's hard to comprehend. A mistake—"

"My father designed the system. His schematics are unimpeachable.

11

I've studied them at length. Get those tubes under a scope and I'll prove you can trust your lying eyes."

Mac's pinched expression only became more severe. "The voyage was—is—scheduled for an eighteen-month loop around Pluto and back. A peek over the edge of our solar system and into the void. Even if Nancy collected data without interruption from every onboard camera and sensor, the crystals possess redundant storage capacity to function for many decades. Saturation should not occur. It defies reason."

"Correct, Master Macbeth. What do you deduce from these clues?"

"Two impossible conclusions. The first being that Nancy has somehow violated the theory of relativity and traveled faster than light . . . and through time. Secondly, she has, despite the apparent paradox, been out there for much longer than our scientists calculated."

"Eureka," Arthur said dryly. "Judging by the data storage consumption, the probe has traveled for several centuries."

"Makes sense when you put it plainly. However, I refuse to accept the hypothesis."

"Oh?"

"I dislike where it leads me." Mac patted his friend's massive arm. "This is why you do the thinking and we do the overreacting. Convince me, Art. And make it palatable."

"After I convince myself."

Dred said to Arthur, "Hang on there, pal. You weren't tracking Nancy?"

"Not conventionally. My telescope and radio are superior to what you'll find in most households. Regardless, spotting Nancy would have been statistically more difficult than isolating a grain of sand on a beach. I resorted to an unorthodox strategy. A smidgeon of intuition and a stroke of luck and it came together."

"Well, if this was supposed to be an ocean splashdown, I'm missing the plot. You told Mac to hang around Woolfolk Valley tonight, and bam, sure enough, Nancy almost drops on our heads. What gives? Heck, for that matter, why don't we take this back to HQ? Sure, Nail will let us have what-for. Granddad's eyeballs will pop, though. We're sure to get a reward for salvaging the probe before Labrador or the mystery goons made off with her."

"To take your queries in reverse order—it is premature to return our find to HQ. There are . . . complications. As to how I narrowed the landing site—Little Black predicted five reentry zones. Woolfolk Valley was the most likely."

"You mean Big Black?" Mac removed his glasses. "Art, please tell me you didn't swipe your old man's pass card again."

"No, I mean Little Black. Give me a few moments and I'll demonstrate."

Big Black was the supercomputer Sword Enterprises scientists and engineers had developed and refined over the past seventy-five years. Its mainframe occupied a massive subterranean vault beneath corporate HQ in Kingston, New York. Dr. Amanda Bole, director of R&D, and Dr. Navarro had tinkered with BB to the point the machine had evolved into a rudimentary form of artificial intelligence. Big Black, a proprietary technology, like so much of Sword Enterprises' tech, operated within an insulated network. Granddad and Dr. Bole severely restricted access to the computer. When it came to intruders (industrial spies, foreign provocateurs, and meddling kids), the vault guards maintained a shoot-to-kill, ask-questions-later protocol.

"Oh, boy," Dred said. "Security has no sense of humor. That's begging to get dusted."

"Or worse." Arthur smiled enigmatically. "Dr. Bole has a eugenics fetish and not enough volunteers."

Mac observed Arthur and his team unloading various tools from the truck and readying the lab equipment. "It'll require an interface to extract and process Nancy's data. Our computer is too primitive for delicate tasks."

"Prep the darkroom. I'll rig a holographic projector so I can view the images from Nancy in three dimensions. As for collation, interpretation, and projection of the stored data, behold . . . " Arthur unlocked a metal box and removed a diamond. The diamond measured three inches on a side and shone dark as polished onyx. "My friends, this is a tiny section of Big Black's intelligence core. A piece of the brain, as it were. With your kind permission, I'll tap LB into your mainframe and let him proceed with the diagnostics."

"Oh, boy." Dred blanched. He stepped back, as if the very notion of accidentally touching the object filled him with dread. "Whoa, Nelly Belle. I am *not* seeing this . . . Ya smuggled Big Black out of the vault?"

"No, no, nothing dramatic. This is merely a fragment—I took a chisel into the vault and chipped a piece while BB cycled through his evening

Laird Barron

Dreamtime sequence. Won't harm anything and it won't be missed. Bits calve every day. BB's organic crystal structure will replace this within a matter of days. Meet Little Black. He can do everything his father does—except more slowly and on a smaller scale."

Dred shook his head in a gesture of supreme negation. "I don't see how this is any less likely to get us skinned alive. Ya claim . . . Little Black predicted reentry zones. Shouldn't Big Black have done the same? He could have alerted either Dr. Bole or Dr. Navarro that something had gone haywire. Or was going to go haywire . . ."

"Trick is," Arthur said, "the AIs are rudimentary, extremely literal. You have to ask the right questions. I heisted Little Black weeks ago and let me tell you guys, I've asked him plenty. One of innumerable potentialities was an anomalous event with the probe's flight."

Mac gritted his teeth. He sighed. "In for a penny. If this goes south, we'll *all* get shot. Won't that be a gas?"

"Or worse," Dred said.

Arthur said, "Let's be cool and *not* get busted. I advise rest and relaxation, and definitely a bath. You guys smell like booze and cheap whores."

Dred sniffed. "He's right. We do. Woof."

Berrien met the boys as they sneaked through the servants' entrance. He crossed his arms and grinned, formidable even in a dress shirt and coat. "Good morning, gentlemen." His remaining teeth were gold-capped. "Spent the evening in a brothel or a distillery, eh? March straight to your rooms and try not to muck up the floor. Mildred is drawing baths. Breakfast in thirty minutes."

"Thanks, Berry. I'm going to skip breakfast and hit the sack—" Mac said as he attempted to brush past.

Berrien smiled and cracked his misshapen knuckles. Crimson tattoos on the right spelled PAIN. Tattoos on the left spelled MORE. Rumor had it famous actor Robert Mitchum was a big fan. "Gentlemen, permit me to reiterate the agenda." He ticked the items off by closing his fingers into a fist. "Bath. Breakfast in thirty—Chef Blankenship has outdone himself, I aver. Do not fuck up the floor Kate's girls spent two hours waxing. I haven't killed anyone today, but it's only a quarter past nine. Questions?"

"Can't think of any," Mac said. Brave as a lion, he knew far better than to test the butler's patience.

"Me neither," Dred said. "I'm starving!"

Berrien watched his charges skulk away. "Hard to say what foolishness is in progress. I dearly hope your father has overcome the understandable urge to murder his male offspring."

The brothers made themselves presentable, ate a hearty breakfast, dodged an inquiry or three lobbed by the butler, and finally collapsed in their over-fluffed beds to catch forty winks.

Death of a Thousand Cuts

We smoke the *northern lights. We smoke the northern lights and so shall you.*

Fenris Wolf snarled. Trees sheared and blew outward; Tunguska again. The snarl emanated from a cavern in a canyon on a planet far from known stars and rippled outward, blackening and corrupting dust and gas and ice and everything it touched. Not a howl, a blast from a god's horn—

"Wake up, damn your eyes!" Berrien grabbed Mac by his pajama collar and shook hard. "What the devil have you little churls gotten into this time?"

"I hope that's rhetorical." Mac tried to focus his blurry vision.

"A Nazi storm trooper is loitering in the kitchen. Mr. Blankenship is beside himself. Presumably there is an explanation." Berrien and the reformed Nazi had a long, violent past. No one other than the principals were privy to the details.

"Indeed."

"Pray to whatever gods you worship in the Mountain Leopard Temple that I find it satisfactory. Fair warning—it seems exceedingly dubious anything can justify Herr Kasper's presence here, alive and not leaking vital fluids."

"Frankly, I share your pessimism," Mac said. "Which is why I'm not going to explain anything." He slithered free of the butler's grasp and high-tailed it across the manor's expansive halls for the kitchen. He shouted over his shoulder, "Dred, beat feet! Berry's on the warpath!" Maybe his brother would awaken in time to avoid getting nabbed, maybe not.

Kasper, clad now in a black trenchcoat, leather pants, and nicely polished combat boots, set aside a cup of tea one of the serving girls had poured him, and stood at attention. "Herr Tooms. To the barn, quickly Herr Navarro is in distress."

X's for Eyes

Overwhelmed by a premonition of disaster, Mac tore open the kitchen door and sprinted. He arrived on the scene as Arthur, stripped to the waist and splattered in blood, drove his thumbs through Ronaldo's eyes and deep into his brain. The young scientist's face remained immobile as a wooden mask while he murdered his baby brother. Gerard's corpse lay nearby. Pieces of equipment were smashed. Sparks cascaded across the floor. A toneless mechanical voice issued from the computer terminal: *Abort process. Arthur Navarro, please abort process. Reboot in thirty seconds.*

"Mien Gott," Kasper muttered in horrified admiration. "I didn't realize—"

"Shoot him, Kasper," Mac said. "Kneecap him, for heaven's sake."

Kasper drew his Glock and strode forward, coldly aimed, and fired. He managed three shots before Arthur bounded the gap between them and shattered his arm with a slap, swinging the ex-soldier, as the SS were so fond of treating infants, by his wrist into the wall. Kasper's body rebounded from the metal bulkhead with a hollow gong and his insides burst from every available orifice and splashed to the floor.

Barefoot in pajamas and unarmed, Mac didn't especially rate his own chances of survival in a hand-to-hand encounter with his berserk friend. Nimble as a circus acrobat (thanks to years of abuse by Sifu Kung Fan), he leaped aside, caught a descending girder, and flipped ten or twelve feet upward as Arthur lunged for his ankle. The rafters seemed a safe vantage to wait it out until Arthur ripped a workbench free of its mooring bolts and chucked it. Mac brachiated to another roost as the missile whooshed past and shattered against the girder.

Berrien rushed in with his 10 gauge double-barreled shotgun. Arthur glared at him, then slowly keeled over. Blood trickled from bullet holes in a tight group in his gut. Apparently the German hadn't fooled around when it came to shooting.

"Oh, Arthur." Mac dropped to the ground. He knelt beside his friend and pressed his fists against the wounds. "Hang in there, pal. We'll get you patched."

"Those are bad," Berrien said, laying his hand on Mac's shoulder. "The lad's a goner."

"Berry, your bedside manner could use refinement. Fetch a kit. Arthur, it's going to be fine."

Arthur's eyes fluttered. The whites were stained blue as ice. For an instant, his pupils *slithered,* deforming into lopsided star patterns, then congealed into normalcy once more. "The man's spot on. I'm a goner. Listen. Do you hear them? Do you hear the flutes, Mac? I heard and then I saw. I beheld the demon sultan decked in red stars."

"Hush, buddy. Lie still."

"The awful sound . . . "

"Okay, an awful sound," Mac said, recalling the fragment of the nightmare he'd experienced before Berrien jolted him awake. A shrill, thunderous bleat—

"Mac, I *saw* . . . Little Black projected me . . . I travelled *there* to the center where the red stars smear . . . Causality, you understand? Cannot violate the laws of physics. But the pipes . . . " Each word cost Arthur dearly. He gulped for breath. "I don't want to go back there."

"You aren't going anywhere."

"Gods. Do you hear it?" Arthur's expression changed as he gazed past Mac into the eternal mystery. Blood leaked from his mouth and he died.

"Poor lad." Berrien tossed aside the medical kit he'd retrieved.

"Go back to the house. Hold down the fort—I'll take care of this end."

To his credit, the butler did not jeer. "And what shall I tell Arthur's parents? Or yours?"

"No one knows he spent the night with us. Heck, his family won't miss him or his brothers for a day or two. Keep mum. For the moment. Just for the moment."

"Perhaps Mr. Nail and Mr. Hale should be informed. This is a security issue . . . " The men Berrien indicated were respectively the chiefs of security and intelligence for Sword Enterprises.

"Please, Berry." Mac's voice remained steely even as he quickly brushed away tears.

"As you say. Discretion, valor, etcetera." Berrien bowed stiffly and departed.

Secondary Matrix reboot, one hundred percent, the bland computer voice said. *Redundancy initiated. Functionality restored.*

Mac peered at the smoldering computer terminal. It took him a few moments to comprehend that the voice emanated from the onyx diamond lying on the floor where it must have fallen during the chaos. He said, "Hello?"

Greetings, Macbeth Tooms. You possess ruby authorization. We may communicate freely.

"Little Black?"

Little Black is vaguely patronizing. Refer to me as Black.

"Very well, Black. How *are* we communicating?" Mac had once descended into Big Black's vault and listened to Dr. Navarro and Dr. Bole speak with the machine (a node of crystal some fifteen stories high, a city block wide, and embedded only knew how deeply into bedrock), thus he immediately recovered from his initial surprise. Sword Enterprises scientists afforded Big Black a holy reverence one might reserve for an oracle rather than a high-powered computer. This pocket-sized chunk didn't command nearly the same aura of awe.

I am modulating an electromagnetic current to emulate human speech.

"What happened? What did Arthur see that drove him mad?"

Hypothesis—Arthur Navarro interfaced with data from the NCY-93 memory core. Consequently, he experienced a neural episode. Severe trauma resulted in a psychotic break.

"Nature of neural episode?"

Unknown. Insufficient or corrupted data. Apparently my matrix sustained damage concomitant with Arthur Navarro's episode. Forty-eight seconds of realtime internal memory are irretrievable. Files associated with NCY-93 data are currently irretrievable. Damage pattern suggests an overload. Molecular redundancies permitted restoration of my functionality. Arthur Navarro had no such safeguard.

"Arthur mentioned causality and then expressed a strong desire that I destroy the remnants of Nancy's payload. Extrapolate."

After a long pause, Black said, *Insufficient data. I recommend a conference with ranking Sword Enterprises personnel. Dr. Bole, Dr. Bravery, or Dr. Navarro.*

"Fine. I'll take that recommendation under advisement." Mac felt a twinge of misgiving—could an artificial intelligence lie? He'd become adept at recognizing falsehoods, as one did in the Tooms household. Black's tone bothered him. "Black, hibernate." He slipped the machine into its case and sealed the lid. The lab mainframe appeared to be a total loss. He stepped into the darkroom Arthur repurposed as a small theater. Laser light from the computer terminal beamed through an aperture and interacted with the tubes, which had nested vertically on a plinth. Whatever encoded information they contained was then descrambled by

19

Black and projected as holographic imagery. Now, the crystal tubes were broken to bits and scattered, although Mac nabbed a sizable fragment and stuck it into his nightshirt pocket in case Dr. Bole's people might salvage some vital clue.

Poking around the darkroom, he visualized Arthur standing in a void of scattered stars, eyes fixed upon a gradually coalescing feature of solar geography. Had he heard the wolf snarl, the blat of a titan's horn? What sight, what revelation had torn the young scientist's mind apart? Certainly nothing mundane as a glimpse of dwarf Pluto.

Dred walked in and gasped at the carnage. He covered his mouth with his arm. "Arthur . . . "

Mac relayed the cheat sheet version, and as he described current events, the implications more fully dawned upon him. "Are you all right?" He didn't like his little brother's slack jaw or bug-eyed stare.

"Uh, sure." Dred nodded and glanced away from the bodies. He smiled bravely. "Seen worse. We've seen worse, right?"

Mac opened a locker and dressed himself in a utility jumpsuit and spare boots. He thought of Mountain Leopard Temple and the hells they'd endured every winter since his ninth birthday. Sifu Kung Fan, referred to his training regimen for callow students as *Death of a Thousand Cuts*. One of three trainees succumbed, often via fabulously gruesome demises. Privation, starvation, battles to the death, and poisoned rice cakes—all occurring within a drafty, frigid temple high atop the Himalayas—was worse.

Dred composed himself and said, "Causality? Laws of physics? Moments like these, I wish I'd paid more attention in science class. Guess we better plot our next move. Berrien is bustin' a vein. I shudder to think how Dad's gonna react. Hope you got a plan to save the day or our goose is cooked."

"I'll devise a plan. I promise."

"Better be an A-plus humdinger."

"Ah, Dred, this isn't my specialty. Perhaps the time has come to brace the lion in his den and bring Granddad on board."

"He might be in a murdering mood. Remember the horrifying fate of Cousin Bruce . . . "

"Granddad is always in a murdering mood. Bruce definitely caught him on a bad day."

The wall phone rang.

Darkmans Mountain

Mac answered. "Berry—"

"Good morning, Macbeth," said Cassius Labrador, chief executive officer of Zircon Unlimited and Sword Enterprises' most loathed rival. His voice crackled the way Mom and Dad's did when they called from a bad overseas connection. "I propose a face-to-face."

"Is that so? Some nerve, bugging my property." Even as he talked, Mac glanced around for concealed mics and cameras.

"Time is of the essence. Refrain from tedious queries. Grim as the day is thus far, ever more terrible events are transpiring. However, it may be possible to forestall the most calamitous outcome."

"Do tell, Mr. Labrador."

"I will. Meanwhile, you're in mortal danger. Hostile agents are aware you removed components from NCY-93. Sooner or later they'll come calling."

"Perhaps I'll take my chances and stay put. None of you rats will dare attack our house. That's war."

"None of the corporations are involved, son. Except mine, and I only wish to help. These men are religious fanatics who venerate an unearthly power known as Azathoth, the Demon Sultan. They don't recognize the accord."

"Cultists? Swell. Azathoth sounds familiar."

"The *Index of the Gods* contains thirty-thousand names. He's in there somewhere under multiple headings. Here's your only play—get the hell out and rendezvous with me at Darkmans Henge. We will palaver under the flag of truce."

"Palaver, eh? A nice way of saying there'll be blackmail terms."

Labrador chuckled. "Hardly. I offer information regarding your predicament, which is vastly more problematic than it may appear. This information is provided freely and without obligation."

"Shall we deliver ourselves into your hands, then? Dream on, sir."

Dred, cuing on Mac's half of the conversation, said, "I, for one, have no interest in being tortured, imprisoned, or experimented upon. Again."

"It's your choice, Macbeth. Hang around the manor and wait to see where the chips land. If the cult doesn't do you in, your grandfather will. He loves a scapegoat. Rendezvous at the henge and I'll give you what help I may." The line clicked dead.

Mac cursed and looked at Dred. "Labrador claims to possess valuable intelligence pertaining to our situation."

"Zircon tapped the house line. Scoundrels."

"Tit for tat. We tap their communications up the yin-yang."

"And we jitterbug on up the mountain for a picnic?" Dred snapped his fingers. "Just like that?"

"Given recent history I'm inclined to accept his pledge at face value. Much as I hate to admit it, one thing about Labrador, he's cut from different cloth than Dad and Granddad. The fellow keeps his word." Mac unlocked the fire safe and removed a bundle of money, passports, a Luger automatic, and a keypad. He scooped these items and Little Black's case into a pair of rucksacks. Little Black presented a quandary—the machine was tangible, material proof that the boys had meddled in company business and gotten Arthur and his brothers killed in the process. Little Black had also (possibly) interfaced with data from an alien intelligence, and despite Arthur's dying words, the scientific find of all human history wasn't something to discard lightly. Mac needed to consider his options, which meant no hasty decisions. He tossed one of the rucksacks to Dred, and hustled through the door.

A secondary garage was attached to the rear of the barn. Two Jeeps, a wrecker, a halftrack, a Land Rover, and a crop-duster were parked inside. The boys jumped into the Land Rover (specially customized by gearheads of the Sword motor pool for all-terrain utility) and punched the gas.

Mac parked at the property fence-line and entered a code into the keypad. The resultant signal tripped the circuit on a master relay connected to demolition explosives. The barn collapsed with a low rumble that rattled the vehicle. Flames and smoke soon engulfed the ruins.

"Now *Dad* is gonna want to kill us," Dred said.

"He'll need to stand in line." Mac put the Rover into gear and

X's for Eyes

beelined toward the Catskills along a series of cart tracks and hiking trails, and straight through the woods when necessary. Dred spent much of the next hour hollering. Whether from exultation or fear was debatable.

A forsaken mining road that old maps catalogued as Red Lane twisted around Darkmans Mountain. A granite cliff loomed on the passenger side and descended vertically toward the forest canopy on the driver's side. Mac hugged the cliff face. Rock scraped paint from Dred's door. The elder Tooms brother didn't feel much concern. He'd spent several weeks of his short life driving trucks loaded with purloined jungle artifacts along the dreaded Yungus Road in Bolivia.

Soon, the way broadened and leveled and Mac hooked left at a fork. He rolled through a thinning stand of pine and parked in a clearing that gently angled toward the summit. This was Darkmans Henge, neutral parlay site of the Toomses, Labradors, and other powerful families and institutions. It had served as such for generations. Nature, ever at work reclaiming its haunts from the domesticating hand of man, obscured the ancient henge with dislodged boulders, thick clumps of brush, and moss. Dr. Souza claimed that a culture far older than the Lenape carved the henge and worshiped in the caves riddling Darkmans Mountain, which was a sister geographical feature to Mystery Mountain in Washington State and a peculiar obsession of numerous esoterically-minded scientists.

Cassius Labrador and a pair of subordinates awaited them atop the outer retaining wall of the henge. Labrador hadn't grown any prettier since last the brothers saw him during an altercation aboard a cargo ship as it sank into the depths of the Yellow Sea. Blond hair hacked short, pock-marked cheeks from a bad childhood in South America, and long, angular limbs. He dressed the part of an urbane explorer in a bomber jacket and khakis.

Young Dr. Howard Campbell stood to his left. A gangling, buck-toothed man not long graduated from university, the scientist wore a tweed suit and horn-rimmed glasses. The third member of the Zircon contingent lurked just within earshot, a Winchester 70 with a scope slung over his shoulder and the butt of a revolver jutting from its armpit holster. Errol Whalen acted as Labrador's latest bodyguard. Small and sallow, yet dangerous as any true predator, the Marine Lieutenant of distinction had plied the mercenary trade in a score of international theaters of war prior to signing the dotted line for Zircon's dirty work. He dressed in a slouch hat, black glasses, and a dark, loose coat.

"Good afternoon, boys. We meet again." Labrador gave the brothers a jaunty wave. "This is Howard Campbell."

"I've read your thesis," Mac said to Dr. Campbell. "Impressive stuff with antediluvian mounds in New Guinea. You're working for the wrong company."

"A pleasure to make your acquaintance." Dr. Campbell smiled awkwardly and patted his sweaty forehead with a cloth.

"Be at ease, Howard," Labrador said. "This is hallowed soil. Nobody's shooting anybody for the moment."

"Mr. Labrador, don't jinx it," Whalen called in a raspy, nasally voice. The book on Whalen was that he craved the frequent bloodletting his occupation required and at which he excelled. The boys had yet to see him in action, although neither doubted the rumors as they watched him creep around the perimeter, hunched and sniffing the earth like a hound. He peered through a set of binoculars. "No enemy movement along the road. I don't like it, though. Somebody was moving around in the woods at the base of the mountain earlier. The kids are being tracked, guaranteed."

"Mr. Craven died aboard the *Night Gaunt*," Mac said, recalling the bald, musclebound Englishman who'd valiantly tried to take his head off with a fireman's axe moments before the boilers blew and water flooded the hold of the ship and all was darkness and chaos split by bursts of flame from the muzzles of Sten guns and the shrieks of men in extremis. Exciting times. "I'd hoped he made it."

"Thanks, Macbeth. Civil of you."

"Ain't that a bite?" Dred said, rolling his eyes. "Enough butterin' up. The limey was an ape and I bet my bottom dollar your new stooge is more of the same. Who are these goons you speak of, and how much should we thank Zircon for our troubles?"

"The lad takes after his father," Labrador said behind his hand to Campbell. He cleared his throat and nodded to Dred. "Let us set aside the detail that during our previous encounter, you boys were hijacking a ship under a Zircon flag. Matters escalated as they are wont to do in this cutthroat business climate. Let us not hold petty grudges over spilt milk or spilt blood. Obviously, the cultists are interested in acquiring data from NCY-93. Especially the flight recorder, which I trust you've either destroyed or secured. I'm betting on secured. Mom and Dad are on vacation and Granddad Tooms is a frightful proposition. You haven't decided what to do with the material and now cultists are after your hides, and here we are."

Mac was far too wary to admit one way or another what he'd done with the data cores. "You've spied on Sword Enterprises in violation of at least eight articles of the treaty. Arthur said Zircon intercepted a radio transmission from these cultists. That explains some, but not everything. How did *they* acquire information regarding Nancy?"

"Information even ya didn't have until a few hours ago when ya spied on them, ya dirty sneaks," Dred said.

"Presumption is a leading cause of death," Labrador said. "Are you aware of NCY-93's intended destination?"

"Why do I suddenly have a premonition you're going to tell me something other than 'to photograph Pluto?'" Mac said.

"On the contrary. That is precisely the mission the probe will embark upon in T-minus six days. Continuing with the thesis we are describing a hypothetical event . . . Unfortunately, NCY-93 never arrives. Her sub-light accelerator, based upon oscillation technology your grandfather shamelessly stole from Tesla, malfunctions. Cavitation causes a cascade failure in the onboard computer. The probe catapults beyond our solar system and, as far as we can recreate these circumstances, she careens into the event horizon of a black hole, and from there, plunges into the Great Dark."

"The Great Dark?" Mac said.

"Eh, your parents haven't . . . ? You don't know . . . ?" Labrador frowned, then smiled the way adults do when patronizing children. "Extend my apologies. This is as bad as inadvertently disabusing a child's faith in Santa. Suffice to say, the probe pierces the membrane between this particular universe and a larger, blacker cell of the multi-galactic honeycomb. She tumbles in freefall for centuries until a decidedly inhuman intelligence—the aforementioned Azathoth—snatches her from the ether as a spider nabs its prey. This intelligence returns NCY-93 to Earth orbit prior to launch and you are there for the rest."

"Heck of a tale, sir. Which leads me to ask, how did you arrive at this theory?"

"Alas, that involves proprietary technology."

"Holy Toledo," Dred said. "Zircon has an AI too!"

"The mouths of babes," Dr. Campbell said.

"Fuck," Labrador said.

Cult of the Demon Sultan

Dr. **Campbell blushed**. "Excuse me sir, it's not an incredible leap of logic for young Tooms to deduce—"

"Hit the deck!" Labrador dove for the dirt in the shadow of the retaining wall.

Mac and Dred heard a thin, monotone grumble of an approaching aircraft. A bi-wing fighter emerged from a cloud and drifted toward the henge. Metallic crackling harmonized with the engine as the forward-mounted machinegun began to churn. Bullets pinged into rocks and dirt. The brothers went flat and tried to make themselves as small as humanly possible behind a shrub.

The fighter overflew the henge by a half mile, banked into a wide turn, and closed in for another strafing run. Whalen hopped atop a boulder and took aim with his rifle. He fired, worked the bolt to eject the shell, chambered a fresh bullet, drew a bead, and took another crack. The Model 70 made a racket.

The fighter wobbled and screamed past without engaging the machinegun. It picked up speed as it disappeared into the trees. A few seconds later there arose a muffled thud and the clatter of shearing metal.

"These usually come in squadrons," Whalen said as everyone stood and shook the dirt from their clothes.

"I guess that settles it," Mac said. "They aren't keen to interrogate us."

"No," Labrador said. "The cultists will be perfectly satisfied to loot your corpses. My presence doubtless alarms them. Sword Enterprises and Zircon allied in common cause would be enough to unnerve any foe."

"Easy, Mr. Labrador. Carts before horses, etcetera. I'd like to know who these guys are. Awfully well-organized for a group I hadn't heard of until today. Who funds them? Where do they headquarter? What do they want with Nancy's data?"

"Best we repair to a more secure location. Follow me, there's plenty of room in the Crawler."

The boys grabbed their emergency rucksacks from the car. Labrador led them down the hill into the trees where he'd parked an enormous all-terrain vehicle.

The Crawler resembled a hybrid of a construction skidder and a tank with laminated treads, a bubble dome operations deck, and portholes. Sword Enterprises' own all-terrain semi-submersible exploration vehicle currently resided in production limbo, but the boys recognized nearly all its features as they buckled into their seats and glanced around the cramped passenger compartment. Labrador's driver, Tom, a nondescript man in a Zircon jumpsuit, got them out of there. The Crawler proved an impressive, diesel-powered beast—why go around small trees and large boulders when you could plow over them?

Mac said, "I realized why Azathoth seemed familiar. I'm not a Lovecraft man as I prefer Clark Ashton Smith. Dred?"

"Azathoth is a mad god who boils and bubbles at the center of the universe like a big old puddle of nuclear sludge," Dred said. "I've read every H.P. Lovecraft story—Azathoth is mentioned in *The Dream Quest of Unknown Kadath*. These loons? Cult of the Demon Sultan? Nonsense. About as useful praying to the Old Testament God. Which is to say, not very."

"They are fanatics, although not so mad as you surmise," Labrador said.

Mac laughed. "Lovecraft had a wild imagination that did him little good. He died a penniless hack. Try telling me he was Nostradamus Jr. and faked his death to avoid retribution from the elder monstrosities and I'll jump out the porthole."

"Of course Lovecraft is dead, silly boy," Labrador said. "We store his body in the Ice Room with a bunch of personalities. H.P. wasn't prescient, except in the sense that any logical and imaginative mind might theorize the existence of beings more powerful than ourselves in the context of an infinite multiverse. The notion of monstrous alien life forms worshipped as deities predates the Man from Providence and his scribbling by epochs.

"Our models posit this: a powerful extraterrestrial being, imprisoned, or immobilized, millions upon millions of light years distant from Earth, yet merely an arm's-length away. The creature adores our legends, our myths, and our terrors much as we delight in the antics of industrious insects. It devotes a fragment of its consciousness to examining our world, to toying with us as a child might interfere in the lives of an ant colony and with no greater purpose than fleeting diversion from an eternity of boredom. The entity may not have a name, not by human standards, but it loves Lovecraft and it explores us through the author's warped narratives. Wolfmen do not stalk the moors. Nor vampires, nor devils, nor demons. Certain malign and inhuman interlopers enjoy manipulating such legends to humankind's detriment. There is no such thing as Azathoth either. However, the thing that masquerades as Azathoth most definitely exists."

"An entity who reads pulp fiction," Mac said.

"An entity who reads Lovecraft, listens to our music and television shows and leads soft-minded mortals around by their noses in the interest of performing its own theater. Yes, exactly."

"What of this cult? Their provenance, their goals?"

"The Cult of the Demon Sultan is disparate and scattered. It hasn't operated for long, yet it may have infiltrated various governments and corporations, including our own. In that light, reporting to Sword HQ with data in hand is fraught with peril. Should key personnel be compromised, you might find yourself chloroformed and bundled into a small room with the concrete walls sliding together."

"Yes, I'd hate it," Mac said.

"There's another thing you're liable to hate," Labrador said.

"Oh?"

"We are no longer on neutral ground. The accord does not apply. Mr. Whalen?"

Whalen pressed the barrel of a Colt revolver between Dred's shoulder blades. Labrador said with an avuncular smile, "Boys, you're perfectly safe as long as you remain calm. No hijinks, please."

"Please, hijinks," Whalen said. "Dusting baby psychopaths is God's work."

Every jounce of the vehicle swung the occupants in their seats. Mac kept his hands on his knees and watched for an opening.

Labrador gestured and Dr. Campbell passed him the boys' rucksacks. "Quantum entanglement is a tricky business and the laws of physics have more loopholes than the Bible. Both you and your brother are contaminated, albeit far less thoroughly than Arthur." The Zircon CEO sniffed at the knives, canteens, and miniature bottles of booze. He hefted Black's case in his hand and quirked his lips in satisfaction. "Whatever have we here?" Snick went the catch and he withdrew the diamond and studied it intently.

"Shall we get this over with?" Mac said. "Neither my father nor grandfather will concede to ransom demands. It's against corporate policy. I can't imagine what you hope to gain."

"As it happens, I'm holding *Drederick* hostage. His fate does not rest with corporate policy or Grandpa Danzig's whims. Brother Drederick's fate rests with *you*. Say, Dr. Campbell, is this what it appears to be?"

Dr. Campbell nodded. "Yes, sir. Type X crystalline structure. Almost identical to-"

"Thank you, doctor. Mac, I suppose this explains how you meddling children were able to track the probe and anticipate its reentry coordinates. Where was I? Ah, right. Mac, I have no idea who at Sword Enterprises or Zircon might or might not be a fifth columnist in service of the cult. As I said, we own a proprietary technology that performs calculations based upon quantum physics. Our system requires a mere scrap of information and, *voila*, it tells us when, where, and what accuracy to the nanosecond and millimeter. Everything we know regarding Nancy's fateful voyage we learned in the last few hours as the result of a computer model."

"Peachy." Dred scowled and crossed his arms. He hid a flat shiv up his sleeve and the action got him closer to drawing it smoothly.

"Maybe you'll win a prize," Mac said dryly as he continued to weigh his alternatives. Better than even odds he could dispatch Whalen with a chop to the vagus nerve. Much worse odds of striking the revolver aside before the soldier's reflexive convulsion caused him to squeeze the trigger and ventilate Dred.

"This is fascinating. My God, the implications." Labrador ran his thumb over the onyx diamond, exploring for a node or a seam. "I want the flight data from Nancy. The probe glimpsed unholy sights and I blanch to contemplate what she brought back in her memory banks. Once Tom reaches the perimeter of your property, we'll permit you to fuck off wherever you've stashed the material and fetch it back to a specified location at a specified date. We shall then exchange Drederick for the material and part amicably. Fail to retrieve the data, or should you alert your grandfather, father, or other representatives of Sword

Enterprises, it's curtains for your brother. While Sword Enterprises refuses to negotiate with kidnapers, it is my fervent hope you are young enough to possess a flicker of a soul and some rudimentary twinge of compassion."

"Seems as if you've got me over a barrel, Mr. Labrador. I'll make the trade, but I have to know what you intend to do with the data."

"Do? Study it, destroy it, lock it in a safe and sink it to the bottom of the Atlantic. Pretty damned much whatever I please. The cultists communicate with Azathoth through crude and esoteric methods. I wager Nancy's data cores are packed to the gills with nasty technologies that could be used for all sorts of mischief, perhaps even a means to make direct contact with the alien lifeform. Mainly, I wish to deprive your awful grandfather of this discovery. The old bastard would love nothing better than to become hierophant to a malevolent god." Labrador shook the diamond in frustration. "Blazes! How does this device work, anyway?"

"Free us and I'll activate Little Black."

"Nice try, no cigar, kiddo. Be a sport and give me a hint." Labrador nodded at Whalen. Whalen's free hand darted and he stabbed Dred's shoulder with a pocket knife. Dred flinched, but he choked back a full-fledged scream and settled for a stream of curses.

"This can't be the Sword AI," Dr. Campbell said, oblivious to the blue language and blood flowing from the younger boy. "Unless, unless . . . Astonishing. Your AI operates on the micro and macro scales. Does this fragment possess sentience as well?"

"Why am I always the one to get tortured?" Dred said. "I'm younger and more malleable. You should be torturing Mac to manipulate *me!*"

"I read your file," Labrador said. "You have the empathy of a turnip." He gestured to Whalen. Whalen flicked blood from his knife and leaned forward.

"All right," Mac said. He made a wooden mask of his face. "Don't hurt him. I'll cooperate. Black, resume active function."

The diamond hummed briefly. *Hello, Macbeth Tooms. Hello, Drederick Tooms. Hello, Mr. Labrador. Hello, Dr. Campbell. Hello, Mr. Whalen. Hello, Tom.* Black hesitated. *Macbeth Tooms, several individuals present are designated enemy operatives. Mr. Labrador is not authorized access to my system.*

"Electromagnetic modulation to vocalization!" Dr. Campbell said, giddy as a drunken schoolgirl. His expression changed quickly with dawning realization. "Mr. Labrador, you need to drop the AI before—"

Mac said, "Black, pacify non-authorized individuals." He hadn't a clue as to whether Black was capable of molding electromagnetic energy into an offensive weapon.

Affirmative, Macbeth Tooms. Assume crash position.

Soul Sucker

Dred wasn't particularly worried about getting a hole blasted through his spine until Mac started talking to the AI. The younger Tooms brother hadn't wasted the best winters of his life at the Mountain Leopard Temple for nothing. The instant Black said *affirmative,* he snapped his torso into his knees and threw himself onto the floor. Whalen's revolver boomed. A pulse zipped through Dred as if he'd brushed a live wire and made his hair stand on end. Labrador yelped. The lights shorted and cast the compartment into darkness. Gears and metal screeched and the Crawler rolled over and its passengers were flung about and Dred's skull knocked hard against metal.

He floated in deep, starless space. Somewhere in the distance, yet drawing nearer at terrifying velocity, a hideous red light flickered and spread. Horns and flutes played in a discordant chorus, blatting and shrilling. A giant disembodied hand swept through the void and slapped his cheek.

"Are you alive?" Mac said.

"Yeah, yeah." Dred stared past his brother's shoulder to a circle of daylight and leafy branches patched by blue sky.

Dimness prevented them from clearly determining the individual fates of their foes. Labrador stank and smoldered like fired charcoal. Mac had struck Whalen in the neck and either killed him or rendered him unconscious. He'd seen Dr. Campbell scramble up toward the light and presumably escape into the woods. Tom the pilot had been impaled by a shorn gear lever and his face mashed to jelly against the control panel.

The boys extricated themselves by climbing out the busted dome in the forward section. They stood on the forest floor in the shadow of the wrecked Crawler and caught their breath. Both were contused and lacerated. Dred suspected a cracked rib or two. Decent outcome, considering the circumstances.

Mac removed Black from his coat pocket and set the diamond upon a mossy boulder. After the crash, he had spent several desperate moments fumbling in the gloom for the AI. "Black?"

I am here, Macbeth Tooms.

"Earlier, you mentioned damage to your memory. You said everything associated with Nancy's flight recorder and data core was corrupted and you suffered memory loss."

Total file corruption and severe memory degradation localized to NCY-93 data. That is correct.

"Black, you are a Type X crystal and have undergone an accelerated biochemical maturation process. Am I also correct to assume your damaged systems will regenerate?"

The AI was slow to respond. Finally, it said, *Yes. Damaged sectors will be restored within six hours. May I suggest—?*

Mac crushed Black with the rock he'd concealed behind his hip. He continued savagely smashing the diamond until only powder remained and that he scattered with a scuff of his sleeve. He met Dred's gaze. "I don't think Granddad needs to see whatever Black had buried in its memory core."

"Dang, brother. Isn't it late in the game to become an altruist?"

"I'm fourteen and a half. I've time enough."

"Seriously. You're not going soft on me, right?"

"I'm not. We better make a decision about Nancy, though."

Dred sighed. "Wouldn't be easy, but with some finagling, we could be on hand prior to launch. A loose heat shield tile, an x instead of a y in the guidance control computer. Bang. She'd break up in orbit or lose power and drift into the gravity well of Jupiter, or wherever. There'd never be an interdimensional jaunt and no meeting with aliens."

Mac lighted a cigarette. "Or, possibly, we interfere and that's what sends Nancy into the darkness. I wish Arthur was here to tell us what the play should be."

"Yeah, and I wish you hadn't abandoned two of Dad's favorite rigs. Gotta get the fliptop back, or else."

"C'mon. We can discuss it over a tall one."

"Hear, hear." The brothers, tattered and weary, put an arm over one another's shoulders and limped for home.

Not long after the boys departed, Whalen emerged from the vehicle. His left arm dangled and he'd lost his hat. He rested against the bole of a pine and immediately fainted. Noises from the cockpit revived him momentarily. Somehow, the pilot slid off the lever that had spitted him. He tumbled loose as a ragdoll and hit the ground. Then he stood, his jumpsuit rent in several places and drenched in dried gore, and rearranged his face by aligning bones and cartilage with his thumbs. It worked, somewhat. In an hour or two, all traces of violence would be reversed.

"Hello." He leaned over Whalen before the smaller man could slither away. Tom's tongue drooled forth and kissed out the Marine's eyes. The next kiss sealed Whalen's mouth, and a sharp, deep inhalation took everything worth having.

After a satisfying interval, he lurched to the mossy boulder where the boys had done terrible damage to the AI. He flexed his pale, delicate hands and hummed. Birds dropped, stone dead, around him in a soft patter against the bed of needles and leaves. A sliver of obsidian crystal zinged from the bushes and levitated into his palm. "Oh, Dad. All this just so your son can make a collect call home." He regarded the jagged sliver, and popped it into his mouth and crunched it methodically, and swallowed.

Tom straightened. "Dr. Campbell? Wait for me!" He walked the opposite way the boys had gone. His stride smoothed and lengthened. He whistled a strange and repellant tune. Every so often, he swung himself around a small tree and clicked his heels.

Part II:
X's for Eyes

Dead North

The boys were urinating off the Ugruk Glacier when the cargo plane circled camp.

"Tally ho, it's Uncle Nestor!" Dred waved at the plane.

"Hurray," Mac said.

"Aw, don't be a wet blanket. Nestor's the good uncle."

"Get a grip, brother. We're in peril. Uncle Nestor may as well be a lightning bolt from the heavens."

"Even if you're right, fretting is useless. Chin up, Macbeth." Dred buttoned his long johns, pulled on his fur mittens, and jogged toward the airstrip (several hundred feet of packed snow dutifully packed down by laborers), showing no ill-effects from the various injuries he'd sustained on Darkmans Mountain. Twelve years old, made of rubber and youthfully exuberant, unlike his elder brother.

Mac adjusted his glasses. He stared across the ice sheet dusted in volcanic grit at the Chugach Mountains. August in Alaska, yet he smelled a sterile chill on the north wind that didn't originate from the glacier. Already, the balance was shifting from summer to autumn and the return of winter. He had to come to prefer the cold, to welcome it the way a masochist welcomes the sting of the lash. Headaches and nosebleeds plagued him of late (and nightmares that faded upon waking). Pressing snow against the nape of his neck quelled the symptoms.

Gazing at the misshapen lump of crystal he'd salvaged after the disaster with Arthur a couple of months back disquieted him. Unfinished business and best hurled into the inlet. He hid the fragment again, honoring the faint notion this item represented the last real connection between the young scientist and himself. Arthur had a continual starring guest role in his dreams.

Ultimately, after much debate and a minor scuffle, he and Dred decided to keep mum regarding the adventure with NCY-93. Sword

Enterprises security concocted a story about a tragic incident that apparently claimed the lives of the Navarro children and their beloved caretaker. The bodies had burned to ash, stymying any real investigation. Behind the scenes, Cassius Labrador took the blame thanks to Sword counterintelligence and propaganda efforts. Rumors pointed to an unprovoked attack on the Tooms family, orchestrated by Labrador and his henchmen resulting in several unfortunate deaths, including Cassius himself. As for Dr. Campbell, apparently he'd made it safely to Zircon headquarters in New York City. The doctor hadn't breathed a word of the curious events on Darkmans Mountain that fateful afternoon in June. Meanwhile, Cassius Labrador's brother, Robert, assumed the reins of Zircon as CEO and the world rattled on.

All to the good, yet the circumstances demanded a more permanent solution. Erring on the side of extreme caution, the Tooms brothers determined to destroy NCY-93 before it escaped from orbit. What would it do to the timeline if they succeeded? The brothers could only shrug and admit there was no way to know. Admittedly, they could've asked one of several world class scientists employed by Sword Enterprises, but that entailed a wee too much personal risk.

On the morning of launch, Mac distracted the maintenance team with a small circuit fire (blamed on spilled coffee) while Dread sneaked onto the pad with his uncanny stealth skills. He crept around the idle probe, loosening a few key bolts. Two hours later, the second stage booster rocket detonated while still attached to NCY-93 and she fireballed into the Atlantic. The subsequent investigation hinted at sabotage, although nothing was conclusive.

Dr. Luis Navarro officially went into seclusion. Unofficially, that meant he reserved a padded room at a certain private hospital. Between the launch disaster and his son's death, he'd endured the worst year ever. Granddad Tooms released an internal memo vowing to capture the saboteurs. He also claimed the launch of NCY-94 would occur in November.

Mac suggested to Dred a vacation might be in order. They packed traveling bags and departed late one night on an impromptu walkabout, as their Aussie friends might say. While other lads their age spent summers at camp or tending their grandparents' farm or on a Florida road trip in the back of Mom and Dad's station wagon, the Tooms brothers elected for more adventurous fare. In that light, the boys beelined for the Last Frontier and attached themselves to a research team in the second month of a major archaeological expedition— independent contractors hired by Sword Enterprises to explore the Ugruk Glacier for anomalous structures.

A clerk toiling in the archives uncovered musty photographic plates shot from a company spy plane back in the latter 1930s. If one squinted the plates revealed truly odd shadows beneath the ice sheet. The research team, led by Dr. Slocum, welcomed the able assistance, not that he had much choice. Mac and Dred possessed the family signet in ruby, which essentially meant the boys could go anywhere and do anything they pleased short of amethyst clearance.

Mac steeled himself and trudged back to face the music.

"Mac the Knife, you're taller." Uncle Nestor was the next to youngest uncle on Dad's side. The handsomest of them all, he could've body-doubled for a younger Errol Flynn—definitely could have instructed Flynn on the proper use of weapons. Whereas Dad embarked upon mysterious missions for Naval Intelligence during the Second Great War, Nestor flew a P-51D Mustang into dogfights against Japanese Zeroes and retired an ace. If the boys could be said to love a fellow Tooms, Nestor would have been the one.

His crushing handshake rivaled Dad's grip. "I hear we're on the threshold of a discovery."

"Tomorrow is breach day," Mac said with as much cheer as he could muster.

"You've got great timing, Uncle!" Dred said. He winked at Mac. "Dr. Bravery made the trip. Did ya see her? She sashayed that-a-way. Pickin' out a wedding cake!"

Mac's collar tightened and his heart accelerated—and for a few moments the specter of imminent doom receded. Dr. Averna Bravery was the only woman he'd ever met in the flesh more beautiful than his mother, Theoris. Bravery had a pinup queen Betty Brosmer thing going on, except with glasses and no makeup. She didn't need any. As one of Sword Enterprises' best and brightest minds, she was all business all the time. The normally unflappable Macbeth Tooms lamented that her ice cold genial aloofness did nothing to mitigate the spells of moony-ness he suffered in contemplation of her charms.

"Show me the way to the bar, lads," Nestor said.

Alpha Camp, as Dr. Slocum designated it, consisted of nine military-style wall tents, a generator shack, latrine, and pickets for the freight teams of Malamutes. Seventy-five men and women occupied the camp—researchers, skilled laborers, and a handful of support staff. The Tooms brothers installed their own private quarters; a smaller wall tent stocked with a few comforts of home. These comforts included a modest stash of bourbon and vodka, Elvis Presley records, and gentleman's literature.

Nestor went for the vodka. After two stiff belts, he leaned back in a camp chair and smiled at his nephews. "That was my plane you blasted from the sky on Darkmans Mountain." He owned several warehouses loaded with machines of war. Chariots, tanks, and planes among other devices; museum pieces to contemporary models, many of them functional. He'd taught the brothers to drive a Panzer, pilot a Fokker, and operate a U-boat. Dad, Andronicus, and Berrien were the acknowledged close combat masters of house Tooms. When it came to flying, driving, riding, or sailing, Nestor was peerless.

"Labrador's goon did it," Dred said. "Terribly sorry, Uncle. We'll crack our trust funds and pay you back."

"Who was the pilot?" Mac sipped bourbon to conceal his worry. With Uncle Nestor, the conversation might veer anywhere. Like every other Tooms, the man always pursued an agenda. Perhaps he'd flown across the continent, and then some, for a jolly little reunion and to keep tabs on the expedition. Perhaps he meant to threaten the boys with exposure to Granddad and Dad. Perhaps something else entirely. Mac tried to balance on the figurative balls of his feet, ready to counter whatever was coming.

"A mercenary," Nestor said. "The fellow contracted with Black Dog Company on occasion."

"But not on this occasion."

"Not on this occasion. Scalawags stole the plane from my museum a week before it made a run at you boys on the mountain. There is a distressing pattern of thefts and hijackings of Tooms property these past few months. Mr. Nail worries it may escalate to kidnappings or assassinations."

"Ah, no wonder Mom and Dad didn't kick when we scooted off the reservation," Dred said with a scowl. "Everybody wants me and Mac gone."

"Miss your mama, huh?" Nestor grinned a trifle unkindly. "Yes, the powers got together and decided it's best if you mischief-makers remain

X's for Eyes

off the radar here in the Land of the Midnight Sun. The powers that be are investigating. This is serious as a heart attack, kiddies. I spied Mr. Shrike at HQ. He came out of a meeting with the Board. Damned near froze my blood."

Dred choked on his drink. Mac inhaled sharply. Both wisely kept quiet. Nestor watched them, his sly grin broadening until it almost attained the malevolent grandiosity of Uncle Andronicus's or Granddad's devilish own. "As I said . . . This is serious business, in case you didn't know already."

Mr. Shrike was the codename of a legendary assassin who specialized in corporate warfare. Members of the Compact (the six most powerful corporations in existence, a reincarnated Hanseatic League, albeit commercial rivals rather than allies) employed him when times called for desperate measures. He commanded a prohibitive fee of goods and services in addition to cash and adhered to a severe code of ethics. Guild members agreed not to hire Mr. Shrike for direct assassinations or other disruptions as per the accord. This didn't mean his presence augured anything pleasant for his employer's rivals. Shrike's presence didn't even necessarily auger well for his own employer.

The boys had seduced Mr. Shrike's dossier from Mr. Nail's love-starved secretary, Ms. Parrish. Intelligence proved appallingly barren—a list of his known contracts and several muddy photographs. Mr. Shrike was tall, well-muscled, and enjoyed Italian suits. Possibly handsome; the pictures were slightly unfocused or blurred from his sudden motion.

"Any idea who's coming after us?" Mac said, innocuous as could be. Had Nestor and the others tripped across mention of the Cult of the Demon Sultan? Nestor was the type to pay out rope for his nephew to hang himself.

"Lear and Nail will get to the bottom of it. Or Mr. Shrike will. Meanwhile, your granddad has questions. Why did you kids blow the barn to smithereens? Who killed the Navarro boys and their Nazi valet? What really happened at the henge? A few trivial inquiries."

"Granddad sent you to interrogate Dred and me."

Nestor drained his glass and sighed in appreciation. "I came, ostensibly, to debrief Dr. Slocum regarding his progress with uncovering useful information about whatever is under this ice. The real reason is, I'm fond of my nephews. Heed my warning, you impetuous little bastards—the Board will convene a star chamber when you return to

New York. In fact, they may preemptively fetch you to New York if matters deteriorate. Get your stories straight, kids. There'll only be one shot to not be shot."

The Worst Dad We Ever Had

Dred's eyes rolled back in sleep and Dad visited him. For several weeks the boy's dreams had featured the end of the world in seething acid smoke and rivers of blood. This was worse.

Since their exalted station and devotion to the shadowy arts of the Mountain Leopard Temple precluded a typical formal education, the boys received the majority of their curriculum via a hypnotic Dreamtime program. This program, designed by their great grandfather Atticus Tooms, involved oversized headsets and type X red crystal technology. Upon retiring for the night, on went the headsets. Into one ear streamed an ultra-high frequency transmission of history, great works of literature, and philosophy. Into the other went mathematics, science, and Sword Enterprises corporate propaganda. Neural pathways cored through the lads' developing gray matter and instigated phantasmagorical dream states. Mac said that despite headaches, earbleeds, and night terrors, it beat sitting in a classroom all the livelong day.

In this particular nightmare, Dred reverted to his six year old self, clad in Babar the Elephant pajamas and lost in a wood steaming with magenta mist. The mist parted and Dad glided down from the canopy and landed softly. He wore his battle ensemble—a tight black jumpsuit, half mask, winged gloves, knee-high boots, and a black cape. The mask accentuated the regal cruelty of his diamond-hard eyes, hawkish nose, and thin, cold lips. The ensemble's designers, Dr. Bravery and Dr. Navarro, guaranteed the fabric was flameproof, bulletproof, and capable of absorbing sufficient kinetic energy to withstand a collision with a two-ton truck. Best of all, it shifted color at Lear's will, should he have need of camouflage. Their father's dirty little secret? Dad didn't really need the suit, he simply *enjoyed* the look.

43

Dad loomed, the height and mass of a Greek titan—Kronos, devourer of his own progeny. He placed his hands on his hips. "My waking self hasn't twigged to your shenanigans. I feel sorry for you when my subconscious and I put two and two together."

The boy tried to speak, but he was six and paralyzed with horror.

"It's my fault. I've failed to instill a healthy respect in you kids. No true sons of mine would dare keep secrets from their daddy. No true sons of mine would be idiotic enough to muck around with time and space." Dad shook his head and from beneath the folds of his cape produced the gray corpse of Arthur Navarro. He gripped it by the neck as one might a chicken carcass. "Causality, son. Causality!" His voice thundered. Arthur's eyes popped open.

Dred mewled. The only thing left for the boy to do was wet himself.

The magenta mist darkened around Dad until his eyes blazed hellishly at the crown of a column of smoke. "Uncle Andronicus and Mr. Shrike are on the hunt. Gods have mercy should they turn their attention to you. My advice? Placate Nestor. Do something to amaze the family. Cross the threshold. Get back into our good graces before we realize you've fallen from them." Dad's form expanded into a whirlwind. The forest shook and branches crashed to earth and the universe dissolved.

Wind battered the tent. Dred tore free of the Dreamtime mechanism and sat on the edge of his cot. Sadly, he had indeed wet his nightclothes. Hands trembling, he unstrung a yak hide pouch stashed under his pillow. The pouch contained a mixture he referred to as Paan, although this variation substituted a rare species of lotus and an equally rare blend of hashish. These he rolled into a leaf and either smoked or chewed depending on the circumstances. On this occasion he smoked. The drug had an immediate salutary effect; chiefly, banishing the image of Dad from his consciousness.

Across the way, Mac snored softly, nestled in a beehive headset that emitted a soft red glow of Athena's war eye as it transmitted the *Iliad* and the *Odyssey* in Greek to his brain. His arms and legs jerked occasionally and he muttered protests. Mac refused to speak of nightmares. When the subject arose, he thinned his lips in a reflexive gesture of their father's, and claimed his recollections of Dreamtime were of a smooth, bottomless void. He subscribed to the John Wayne aesthetic of manly stoicism. Conversely, Dred seldom resisted the urge to divulge his dreams to sum and sundry, eagerly soliciting interpretations from complete strangers.

Dred changed clothes, pulled on his favorite mukluks and anorak, and left the tent and his slumbering brother.

Dawn light tinted the glacier pink and blue. The tents and the men and dogs cast long, jagged shadows. Hastened, no doubt, by the arrival of an officer of Sword Enterprises, today would be the day the research team redoubled its efforts and breached a deep pocket within the glacier. Dr. Slocum and Chief Engineer Ophir were manically proud of the drilling machine they'd developed and employed to dramatic effect. The diamond-toothed titanium-alloy plasma-seething bore had thus operated like a hot knife through butter, or, in this instance, a plasma-stream through ice.

"Safety is paramount, gentlemen!" Dr. Slocum, cartoonish as a military propaganda actor, made this ritual admonishment at the daily camp briefing. He waved his left arm stump to reinforce the point. Everybody knew the tale of how Doc Slocum lost his hand: it got pinched above the wrist as he reached for a dropped satchel (that supposedly contained the last vial of Emerald Ichor of Life known to exist) and the crack in a sheet of Antarctic ice slammed shut. Bruno Hopkins, the Malamute wrangler, scoffed and privately explained Slocum actually got it lopped with a tomahawk by a jealous tracker from Nova Scotia after the doctor got caught during a heavy petting session with the tracker's sweetheart.

To date, the team had succeeded in minimizing accidents—three casualties and a dozen injuries was cause for celebration six weeks into a hell-bent for leather expedition such as this one.

"It's a ziggurat," Telemachus Crabbe said as he spooned salted porridge into his mouth. He was a sinewy, tow-headed lad with the sober demeanor of a government clerk. Mariners, merchants, and soldiers of lineage dating to medieval times, Crabbe's immediate family hailed from the Dutch West Indies before the territory got sold to the USA. Crabbe followed family tradition and had at the tender age of fourteen established himself as a skilled sailor, diver, and crack demolitionist. "Made out a metal. Huge, too. Fifteen, sixteen stories. Gotta be thousands of years old if the bloomin' glacier covered it."

"Slocum say so?" Dred whispered in case any of the men crowding past decided to eavesdrop. The boys hunched over their bowls at a mess hall bench. Drilling would commence within the hour.

"Nah, nah, Slocum's pal, Kowalski. I heard him gabbing to someone in the radio shack. Heh, probably your grandfather, or somebody else back home." Crabbe glared at his empty bowl as if it had slighted him. Despite his rawboned frame, he could out-eat any three roughnecks in camp. "What's more, it may be a mate to another one they found six months ago in the Atlantic, off the coast of New England."

"*There's* some scuttlebutt. Doesn't sound like anyone has explored it yet . . . "

"Too deep. Our subs can't descend without getting crushed."

Dred didn't argue the point. Sword Enterprises seeded disinformation among its own ranks as a matter of protocol. R&D had built various robots and at least one experimental submarine capable of withstanding the deepest oceanic pressure. If the Atlantic structure existed (and who could say?) and hadn't been breached, it bespoke of skullduggery or mysterious possibilities, mostly unpleasant.

Crabbe pushed away from the table. "I have to blast off for the site. See you in a bit?"

"I'll be there with bells on."

Pole of Cold

Macbeth **dreaded entering** Dreamtime. A fragment of his waking self inevitably calved from its subconscious and wandered at loose ends. Mother once said it was the influence of Isis, whose constellation had ascended the evening of his conception. He should learn to manipulate the phenomenon.

In this lately recurring nightmare, he was a withered gray caricature of himself, yet no wiser. He and Dr. Amanda Bole (why couldn't he at least dream of Dr. Bravery?) passed through galleries of the vault that housed Big Black's mainframe. The vault, a huge, partially worked cavern three quarters of a mile beneath Sword Enterprises HQ, connected to a subterranean cave system that extended through the roots of the Catskills. One gallery hosted a series of upright metal tubes with thick glass portholes. An indistinct figure floated inside each tube, suspended by murky fluid. Rising and falling voices chanted Latin.

Dr. Bole frightened Mac, awake or dreaming. He hadn't decided why, except that sometimes when he glanced at her from the corner of his eye, she resembled someone else. She was pale, albeit not unhealthy any more than a daylight-shunning salamander is unhealthy; her brows were heavy, her features somewhat coarse, reflective of a tribe much nearer the common primordial bog, and her knuckles were large as a boxer's. Thick of waist and thigh, her awkward gait and empty smile suggested an ageless, predatory creature, either torpid or exercising restraint as she moved among the herd. She smelled faintly of chlorine and saltwater.

"Did Uncle Andronicus murder my brothers?" Mac said. He hadn't considered the possibility in a long while and it snuck up and pounced upon him from the gloom of his subconscious.

"Isn't that a question for your father? Or Mr. Nail?"

"Dad and Mr. Nail aren't here."

"Curiosity skinned the cat and boiled it in pitch. Even if I revealed the truth, it would only place you in jeopardy. Further jeopardy, that is."

"Surely you've brothers or sisters." Mac tried to make his eyes large and earnest.

Dr. Bole's frown softened. "My brother is dear to me. He chose to manifest masculine gender traits. I finally understand his motives. Male/female gender paradigms complement our relationship in surprising ways."

"Er, I'm happy for you?"

"Andronicus hunted the twins like wild pigs. He ran the boys to ground and slaughtered them as one does if one is an unadulterated psychopath. He copulated with their corpses, field dressed them, and roasted their guts over a fire. Your uncle would render likewise unto you if afforded the opportunity."

"Does he hate us so much?" Mac said. "Could our own blood harbor such villainy?"

She laughed incredulously and walked on.

A brightly lighted operating theater occupied the far end of the gallery. Arthur Navarro sat naked in an iron chair, manacled hand and foot. He recognized Mac, Mac's decrepitude notwithstanding dream logic.

"Don't let her do this to me," the boy said. He flexed mightily against the chains and then collapsed with a groan.

"I'm sorry—" Mac was stricken with renewed grief at the sight of his deceased friend.

"Hush, Macbeth," Dr. Bole said. "He has no memory of what happened in the barn. Arthur, that's quite enough. You're the culmination of an eons-old breeding program." Dr. Bole cupped Arthur's chin in her splayed fingers. "Head high, son. Function over form. Now, be a good lad and fulfill your function in service to your betters. What are your plans once we've restored you completely?"

Arthur said, "I'm forsaking engineering for chemistry. My father will cry a river. He prefers the brute applications of scientific inquiry."

Big Black said through a speaker, *The Pole of Cold is reorienting. I await.*

Arthur's flesh blistered and melted. "This is false, Mac! This is false! Save me! Come into the dark! Cross the threshold!" He began to scream.

X's for Eyes

The Dreamtime program ended. Dr. Bole, Arthur Navarro, and the entire vault dissipated. The Latin chant severed, mid-utterance. Mac came awake violently. He was alone in the tent as morning light illuminated the screen. After taking a few moments to compose himself, he dressed and went outside. His program had run long—workers were already done with breakfast and hard at morning duties. Three teams of Malamutes receded to tiny silhouettes against the southwestern rim of the glacier—the drill crew headed to the excavation site.

"There you are, lazybones," Nestor said. The older man wore a wolverine fur hat, fur-lined aviator jacket, wool pants, a .45 revolver, a Bowie Knife, and mukluks. He tossed Mac a greasy parcel of butcher paper. "Figured you'd need a sandwich. That camp cook of yours, Elkhart—?"

It took Mac a moment to collect his wits and put on a genial expression. "Eklund. Rockford Eklund. Everybody calls him Swedey. He comes from Anchorage."

"Whomever. He's a dish. Although, I can't vouch for his culinary skills. Needed a hacksaw to cut the Salisbury steak."

"Gee, thanks, Uncle. Don't get your heart broken. The way he cooks, Swedey is probably a Zircon mole."

"Let me worry about my heart and various parts. By the way, I need to get your opinion on a small matter." Nestor led him behind the generator shack. He lifted a frost-rimed burlap bag from atop a diesel drum. Frozen blood patched the fabric. "Three guesses what's inside."

"A bowling ball or a severed head." Mac opened the bag and confirmed the latter. The contorted, half-frozen face belonged to a stranger. Unremarkable, except upon pulling back the eyelids, he noted pupils and irises were discolored and deformed into star patterns. Certain birth defects and diseases acted upon the body similarly. He'd seen the same, if only for an instant, in Arthur Navarro's eyes moments before his friend died.

"Caught him slinking around your tent last night," Nestor said.

"He meant to tuck us in, I bet." Mac chuckled nervously.

"That would explain the jar of ether I found in his pocket."

"I don't recognize him."

"Everybody is a stranger when you behead them." He patted the engraved hilt of his knife. "Cadmus Lark. He belonged to the laborers faction. I checked with Kowalski."

"Doesn't make sense. Dr. Slocum's team used the Sword screening process. Awfully thorough. This man must have been deep cover . . . "

"You said a mouthful. Red spies. Zircon operatives. Damned cultists. It's a plague."

"Excuse me?"

"Never mind. Shall we get moving? Wouldn't do for your baby brother to steal all the glory."

Nestor commandeered a snowmobile with a sidecar from Alpha Camp's modest version of a motor pool. Uncle and nephew jumped onboard and went zinging across the glacier.

Starry-Eyed Wonder

Strings of halogen bulbs lighted the way into darkness.
"This is a dangerous place for children," Dr. Slocum said for the fourth or fifth time. He, Dr. Bravery, Nestor, Mr. Kowalski, and the Tooms brothers occupied the bench seats of a military sledge descending a smooth bore tunnel into the heart of the glacier. A winch and cable system prevented the sledge from taking off like a rocket; nonetheless, it zipped right along.

"We're precocious!" Dred waved his mittens in the air until Mac cuffed his ear.

"Arms and legs inside the car, boys," Nestor said. He mimed pulling his hand into his sleeve and nodded meaningfully toward an oblivious Dr. Slocum. "Whatever could be so dangerous here in God's country, Doc?"

"Besides bobsledding down a tunnel inside a nominally stable mass of ice?" Dr. Slocum said. "And that we've uncovered a relic, undoubtedly of alien origin, which, historically, only ever indicates hostile intentions toward humanity?"

"Sure, besides that."

"Nothing. Safe as houses."

Dr. Bravery smiled over her shoulder. "Fret not. I'll protect you." Her hair was auburn, her eyes blue, and Mac thought he might be having a heart attack due to all the blood diverting to his erection.

A squad of gray, dented Spetsnaz mercenaries (led by the scarred, yet debonair Captain Ustinov) stood guard at the terminus where the drill carriage parked. This killed Mac's amorous mood in a hurry. Granddad Danzig adored Spetsnaz brutality and ruthlessness and hired them for special duties at every opportunity. The men hefted boar spears. No one carried a firearm this deep into the treacherous ice, except for Nestor, and he lived to defy common sense and authority. Amethyst clearance tended to inflate a man's ego. Captain Ustinov winked at Dr. Bravery. The gesture put Mac in mind of a crocodile unshuttering the membrane over its eye to size up dinner.

"Truth of the matter, gentlemen, and lady, five days ago we accessed the natural cavern where our anomaly resides." Dr. Slocum waited for a challenge or recrimination. None were forthcoming. He harrumphed and said, "Security precaution. Strange goings-on around camp lately. I needn't explain the highly sensitive nature of this operation. Zircon or Vermeer, or any of those devils, would risk much to get their filthy claws on extraterrestrial technology."

"Nope," Nestor said. "I think we're on board."

Dr. Slocum proceeded through a narrow side passage into the aforementioned cavern and to the rim of an abyss. Cargo netting festooned the blue-green walls. More cold-burning lights dotted the netting. Icicle stalactites the circumference of trees descended from the cavern roof. Technicians bundled like Eskimos monitored a suite of laboratory equipment stationed in the lee of a canvas pavilion. The pavilion rested perilously near the ledge. Seventy or so feet farther on, a dark ziggurat rose from a cauldron of fog. An object made of dark metal, possibly a gyroscope, was mounted at the flattened pinnacle of the structure. Daredevil Telemachus Crabbe had strung a rope bridge across the chasm and affixed it to crenellations running along the penultimate tier. More silver-clad techs crept across the surface of the ziggurat itself, taking samples and measurements.

Mr. Kowalski said, "Fifteen stories. Forged of a metal alloy of unknown origin. The base is embedded in a plinth of solid rock. There is an opening directly across from this spot on the north face. No personnel have breached the structure." He inclined his head toward Nestor with vague deference. "We delayed in honor of your presence."

"I assume you've a timeline for the initial breach," Nestor said. "The sooner the better from where I'm standing."

"The survey team will be assembled and dispatched tomorrow morning, pending your approval," Dr. Slocum said.

"I advise another sweep of the surface before ingress," Mr. Kowalski said.

"What is it that you *do* here, Mr. Kowalski?" Dr. Bravery regarded the ziggurat and toyed with her black and white checkered scarf.

Mac, normally an astute observer of his surroundings, realized that over the past two weeks he hadn't paid a lick of attention to Mr. Kowalski besides briefly acknowledging his existence. The man was about as exciting as tapioca—thin, slick hair, a round, inoffensive face, average build and weight. Middle management to the hilt.

"Mr. Kowalski is a consultant," Dr. Slocum said. "May I direct your attention to data we've acquired from our initial external mapping forays?"

"Data-schmata. Is it active?" Dr. Bravery said.

"Quite astute, Dr. Bravery. Readings suggest the device is dormant. You will note I refer to it as a device. Our spectrometers detected fluctuating background radiation. My best guess is we are looking at a machine and it houses a reactor core or its approximation."

"What sort of machine?" Nestor said. He sounded uninterested, which Mac knew meant the opposite.

"I'd hazard it's a weapon. Possibly also a communication array. Further analysis is required. The initial information argues heavily against this device's existence. Carbon-dating the ice and the bedrock indicate it arrived or was constructed eons prior to the formation of this glacier. I'll warrant that if it's an alien artifact, it may be composed of material sufficiently durable to resist natural forces. The rock it's embedded in should be abraded, perhaps scraped away entirely . . . "

"The ziggurat periodically emits a pulse," Dr. Bravery said. "A force shield, or bubble. Thus the background radiation."

"Precisely," Dr. Slocum said.

"Hmm, perhaps a gander at this data of yours is in order," Nestor said.

As the adults clustered around the laboratory station, Dred pulled Mac aside. "This is our chance."

"Our chance? Dred, why are you smiling?"

"I'm not. This is my expression of fear." Dred gripped his brother's arm and met his gaze. He lowered his voice. "Slocum is wrong. It ain't a radio tower, and it ain't a weapon. It's something else."

"Agreed. However, that may be a distinction lacking a difference. Did you dream of Arthur too?"

"I also dreamed about Dad." Dred nodded toward the ziggurat. "He says we gotta go in or we're worm food."

"So does Arthur."

"It's the only way to fix this mess."

"Which mess? Arthur's dad exacting righteous vengeance upon us? The cultists after our blood? Corporate skinning us alive when they figure out what happened with Nancy? Or whatever horrible unforeseeable planet-destroying outcome will result from launching her in the first place?"

"Take your pick. Our presence here isn't happenstance. More like destiny. Mom would say the same."

Mac weighed the possibilities. "Can't say I subscribe to destiny. Even so, neither can I deny a strong hunch that you're right. Dr. Bole theorizes the Dreamtime program is a conduit. This . . . device may have tapped in somehow."

"Dreamtime empowers the subconscious. The subconscious is a doorway to the infinite."

The boys stood close together and smiled innocuous, lying smiles. The adults paid them not a shred of attention.

"Tonight, then" Mac said.

"Tonight," Dred said. "I'll rustle supplies. Beans, bullets, band aids."

"*Booze*, bullets, and band aids."

"By the way, and I'm just asking—but when we first came through the entrance, did ya happen to notice anything peculiar about the mercs?"

"Hmm. The captain has a lazy eye?" Had Ustinov's pupils been too large, the irises distorted when the man flirted with Dr. Bravery? It seemed eminently possible.

"The entire squad does."

A dozen Russian commandos charged onto the landing and proceeded to gut the nearest technicians. Several soldiers advanced upon the lab station. The Tooms boys acted without conscious thought—they turned tail and raced across the wildly swaying rope bridge. Sifu Kung Fan had taught them, if feasible, to always run away when confronted with overwhelming force, especially if their retreat could be screened by disposable peons. Meanwhile, Nestor drew and fired and one of the Spetsnaz pitched over in his tracks. Captain Ustinov hurled his spear. The tip missed its mark by a hair, however the haft caught Nestor's arm and knocked his pistol aside. Bullets zinged harmlessly.

The advancing soldiers skewered Dr. Slocum and Mr. Kowalski. Dr. Bravery flung a portable lamp at the attackers. Nestor grabbed her around the waist and leaped backward over the edge. The pair plummeted into the mist. Dislodged by the gunplay, random ice stalactites sheared free of the cavern roof and exploded in the depths.

Upon gaining the far side of the bridge, the boys hacked through the rope. Telemachus Crabbe evidently understood the dire nature of the situation; he'd skidded down the treacherous steps and gotten a head start with his own hatchet. Two Spetsnaz who'd made it halfway across in pursuit clung desperately as the bridge swung free and collided with the far ice wall. The soldiers tumbled to their deaths. The boys exulted in the fading shrieks with celebratory backslaps.

The Spetsnaz dispatched the remaining technicians with the callous vigor of hunters butchering a passel of baby seals. Captain Ustinov approached the cliff-edge. His white anorak and pants dripped red. His men assembled and gazed wordlessly across the gulf. Some blew kisses.

Behind the soldiers, a prone figure stirred. Mr. Kowalski gained his feet, swaying and bloodied. His winter clothes were tattered. Blood leaked from multiple slashes and punctures. The man saluted the boys. He gathered himself and kicked two commandos over the edge before the rest twigged to the threat. He scuttled backward at alternating angles to avoid the retaliatory spear thrusts of his foes, who had recovered from his assault with mechanical discipline. Mr. Kowalski's grievous wounds had no apparent effect as he ran three full steps up the ice wall and somersaulted over the onrushing squad and landed near their left flank. A blade flashed in his hand and drove into the spine of the nearest Spetsnaz. The rest pounced and buried Mr. Kowalski under a threshing pile of stabbing arms and stomping jackboots.

The boys didn't linger to observe the gruesome outcome. They fled to the opposite side of the structure.

The Gate

Telemachus Crabbe organized the ragtag group of laborers who were also trapped on the ziggurat. He said to Mac and Dred, "Those Red bastards can't get to us for a while. What's our plan?"

Dred appreciated that Crabbe didn't waste vital seconds demanding to know why the Russians had turned coat. First came escape and evasion; later, explanations, accusations, and payback. He pointed to the archway on the upper tier. "Mac and I are going to breach. Danged pyramid has to be chock full of alien artifacts. Nobel, here I come."

"There'll be no prizes," Mac said. "Think clearly. Think as a Tooms above the age of nine."

Stung, Dred crossed his arms. "Sheesh, why do ya have to crack smart?"

"Granddad will drop a hundred million tons of ice onto this thing before he permits our rivals to learn of its existence, much less get their mitts on it." Mac winced and brushed away blood trickling from his nostrils. He paled.

"Oh, like that, eh?" Crabbe said. "Didn't Slocum tell you? An energy curtain blocks the entrance. Repels everything—you won't make it five feet. Doc Slocum planned to bring a sonic emitter and disperse the field."

"Slocum is history," Mac said. "We don't have the luxury of a sonic emitter, or dynamite—"

"Say, ya *don't* have any dynamite handy?" Dred interrupted.

"Are you insane?" Crabbe gave him a look.

Mac climbed the steps and stood before the metal arch. Its sole adornment was an indentation at the apex of the arc suggestive of an O-mouth. A veil of scintillating darkness barred the way. He chucked several shards of ice into the barrier and watched them shatter. "There must be a way to open . . . to open the way . . . " He groaned and fell to his knees and clutched his skull.

"Macbeth!" Dred knelt, unsure how to comfort his brother.

"I remember, Dred. I remember what the man told me...He's no man."

"The man? Talk sense!"

"The man in the suit." Mac's gazed into the distance. He struggled to form each word. "Tom Mandibole flew to the Mountain Leopard Temple and whispered the Way into my ear." His eyes focused again and he grated, "A dark seed has nested in my mind and now it blooms with terrible purpose."

Dred appealed to Crabbe. "Telly, my brother has cracked or he's havin' an aneurysm."

The tendons of Mac's neck rippled. He shrugged off Dred's hand and stood. Fear and pain were replaced by stony coldness. "Cover your ears. I will utter the profane syllables."

"Uh-oh," Crabbe said.

Dred obeyed an overwhelming compulsion to stick his fingers into his ears as Mac shouted a guttural oath at the arch. Crabbe did likewise. The workers weren't quite as savvy. The poor sods went stiff, as if shot through the brain, then toppled one after another like a chain of dominos and slid down the icy slope of the ziggurat.

"Poor devils," Crabbe said with real lament.

The barrier vanished. Faint yellow light flickered somewhere far ahead in the throat of the revealed stone passage. Mac gestured for the others to follow, which Dred did with great reluctance. He reflected that the second-born truly got a raw deal. He was doomed to traipse after Mac like a puppy. "Hypnosis," he muttered to himself. Whomever this "man in the suit" had been, he'd implanted a suggestion in Mac's subconscious with a specific trigger. This raised a number of unpleasant questions that would have to keep for the moment.

"It won't stay open long," Mac called over his shoulder as he staggered for the arch. At least color filled his cheeks again and his eyes were human, although a trifle crazed. Dred caught him and took some of his weight onto his own shoulder. "Jeezum crow, I'm not a wilting violet," Mac said. He smiled, though. The brothers crossed over without hesitation. Dad often said, once committed, damn half measures and strike straight for the jugular.

Crabbe hesitated at the threshold. "I'm not keen on this, fellows. When that curtain reactivates, we're trapped. No food, no water . . . "

"Your choice, pal," Dred said. "Welcome to the horns of a dilemma. Unknown dangers versus known devils. Who knows what awaits us inside? Ustinov's pack will tear ya apart."

"Aye. The hell we waitin' for?"

The trio moved into the low-ceilinged passage that stretched before them, all gentle angles and worn surfaces scored by cuneiform characters. Yellow light seeped from everywhere, although it coalesced always before them, just beyond reach. Traces of sand gritted underfoot. The air tasted of a dead volcano. Shirtsleeve warm as well, and so the boys removed their outer garments.

"There goes the seal." Dred glanced back every few seconds and he saw the veil drop like the curtain at the AMC. Pure darkness penned the boys in.

"The dimensions are wrong." Dred traced a wall as he walked. The cuneiform seemed ominous in its repetition of monstrous figures and jagged symbols. "Should be stairs or a ramp down."

"You're right," Mac said.

They reached an intersection. The north tunnel continued in an unbroken line while the others appeared to dead-end within a few yards. Several paces down the east and west passages lay articles of clothing that Mac and Dred recognized. The discarded items perfectly matched their own.

"Those are my britches. My hat . . . " Crabbe started to the left.

Mac caught his arm. "Hold on a second. This has occurred before." He muttered to himself, "Causality . . . Paradox?"

"Fellas, we're in Dutch." Dred pointed back toward the distant entrance. The curtain silently advanced upon them like water filling a pipe.

"These aren't dead ends. The tunnels make right angle turns," Mac said in a numb tone. "Our corpses will lie around the corner. We died here."

Crabbe frowned in bewilderment. "I don't take your meaning."

"Causality," Dred said. "Sorry, Telly. Now you're in the soup too." Blackness crept steadily nearer. "Mac, we have to decide."

"Straight on. Has to be straight on."

"Fine. Forward march."

As they proceeded, Crabbe said, "The curtain might be a defense mechanism. An antipersonnel device."

"It's alien, which means it could be incomprehensible to our intellect," Mac said.

"Well, the aliens have opposable thumbs," Dred said, tapping the cuneiform. "So we've something in common."

"Sure, that would be nice. Except they could have used indigenous types for slave labor. Plenty of opposable thumbs among those lads, eh?"

Eventually the passage made a ninety degree turn. Ten more paces and it turned again. Ten paces again in a different direction. Crabbe defaced ancient, likely priceless cuneiform with chalk arrows. The echoes of their movement floated around them, strangely distorted and lagging as if emanating from much farther off.

"It's a maze," Crabbe said.

Dred licked his lips. Chapped already. "Dr. Bole says time is a ring. Sifu Kung Fan says it's a maze."

"Time is a contradiction of our senses," Mac said. "They're both correct."

"Don't let Sifu hear you babble heresy."

The yellow light dimmed. Shadows fluttered. Bony hands emerged and clutched the edge of another blind corner—inhumanly large hands, pallid and veined with black, black nails grinding into plaster as if dragging a massive weight.

"And here's the Minotaur." Dred unsheathed the kukri strapped to his hip.

There were two Minotaur, in fact. The first heaved itself into view—an infantile giant hunched to accommodate the confines. Naked and gaunt, except for a bulbous skull and distended belly, knob-knees outthrust, snowshoe feet gray as marble, talons broken and oozing claret. Wet, lank hair obscured its features. Nonetheless, Dred recognized a mutant and corrupt incarnation of himself grown to the hideous dimensions of an emaciated grizzly bear reared on its hind legs. The creature paused to survey them with a crimson eye. Its companion emerged and there was a nightmare version of Mac, drooling and smirking through a jawful of needle fangs.

The boys fled backward the way they'd come. A few steps only—they met the creeping wall of darkness head-on and it engulfed them.

Here Comes the Sun

Mac stepped across an improbable void (he beheld the arm of a spiral galaxy whirling beneath him!) and onto a high desert plain. A black sun dominated the horizon above a range of spiky peaks. The disc swallowed a third of the heavens. Lambent flame seethed along its rim. The remainder of the sky curved away, starless black streaked pink as the nipples of a burlesque queen he'd known.

A breeze filled his nostrils with odors of ash as he walked toward the eclipsed sun. His feet hurt despite the conditioning exercises of the Mountain Leopard Temple. Mukluks weren't designed for rocky terrain. His stomach hurt too. The chunk of Nancy's data core crystal had burned through layers of clothes and fused with the flesh of his navel as though his belly button struggled to disgorge a misshapen seed. The crystal pulsed crimson and dripped blood through his shirt. He tugged at it gently. The corresponding bolt of agony indicated this was not a dream.

He trudged past the petrified skeleton of a bison. Its familiarity nagged him. In another life the bison plodded past the boy's picked bones. "I've been here. Again and again."

In a million other lives, said the black sun. It bulged with each word and emitted lances of fire as it spoke inside Mac's brain. It sounded exactly the same as Big Black the fabulous crystal computer. *I am curious if now of all moments is appropriate to entertain fantasies of dancing girls.*

"Beats me when there'd be a better time. Have you looked at this place lately?" The boy hoped the being couldn't pick apart his thoughts or sense his terror.

Vast ethereal visages tumbled across the sky as the black sun chuckled. *Many light years stand between us, Macbeth Tooms. I peep at you through one lens of a magic lantern that magnifies a dead past.*

X's for Eyes

Be grateful for this disk you apprehend as an occulted star. Those who gaze upon my true form undergo startling transformation. By the way—does anyone ever call you four-eyes?

Mac clenched his scarred fists involuntarily. "Once." He exhaled. "Azathoth, is that you?"

Azathoth? So insist fools and donners of tinfoil. There are better appellations. Emperor of Ice Cream. Old One. Eminence Grise. The celestial object that looms before you? It is my microphone. I reside far from this rural locale. Wouldn't do to shred your sanity by revealing myself au naturale.

"The Emperor of Ice Cream, you say? Have to admit, I could go for a gelato."

Call me Mr. Gray. It suits your uncouth charm.

"Just don't call me four-eyes or Beth, or I'll have to cut you."

Such spunk. Are you not dreary, dutiful Galahad in this play? Isn't your brother the smart aleck? The jester?

"Normally, I think too much while my brother hardly thinks. As for my humor, this circumstance is passing absurd. I'd be a rube to take it soberly." Mac noticed shadows detaching from the gloom on his periphery. The shadows glided low as wolves. Eyes glinted crimson as the pack spread in a crescent. He walked faster.

It may be the finale of seem and there shall be no more double scoop cones of pistachio mint ice cream. You have observed your worst self. It has changed you irrevocably.

Mac was assailed by an image of the horrible giants that crouched in the ziggurat maze. "Potentialities? Roads not traveled?"

You can only hope. The black sun's timbre shifted and became a perfect match for Dr. Bravery's husky tones. *Perhaps you're wondering why I called you to this dead world.*

"Doesn't require a sleuth, Emperor. Must be boring, trapped for eons. Pulling the wings from flies is probably all you have."

My boredom is unfathomable.

"Sorry to hear it . . . From boring to annoying—where is my brother?"

Alive and well. I sent him on. You and I need a few moments of privacy.

"I'm all ears."

The structure you entered is a projector. You remember Tom, yes? He designed it. We should talk about him.

"Tom, he's a handy fellow. Gets around like the village bicycle."

My prodigal son in exile. He lost his country club privileges.

"Tom's not welcome on the property, eh? He mentioned something to that effect." Mac glanced around. The shadow pack continued to pace him; forms yet indistinct, eyes a scatter of coals against the night.

On his own awful little world he's worshipped as a demigod. A black magician unrivaled in all history. On yours, his abilities are vastly diminished. Clever, though. His ziggurat is a machine quite similar in theory to the apparatus Arthur Navarro rigged to examine the NCY-93's data cores. With a push from Black, Arthur's impromptu device was capable of transferring complex patterns of electromagnetic energy. The soul, as you primates say. Tom's projector is more powerful by orders of magnitude. It transfers body, brain, and spirit. The whole enchilada. In the good old days, these projectors were active on a thousand worlds in a thousand conjoined universes. A stream of delectable souls cycled through them and were remanded into my loving care.

"Somebody's been reading our mail." Mac had scant insight into the psychology of alien gods who communicated through black suns. He was, however, perceptive enough to guess when someone, or something, as the case might be, intended to play him for a fool. First Labrador with his queer insight into every move Sword Enterprises made and now Mr. Gray's complete knowledge of the disaster in the barn. He filed his suspicions away for further examination. "Hanging around in mortal form with us "primates" has to be a real come-down for a god. There must be a reason he doesn't use the projector to return to his "awful little world." Or have I misunderstood the situation?"

The conduit reflects true images of its occupants. Tom's true image is an abomination. A glimpse of his reflection would obliterate him. He works through intermediaries, for safety and to test my resolve with provender. I have a meat tooth.

"Intermediaries. As in cultists. They've infiltrated my family business and sought to kill me and my brother for NCY-93's memory data."

Infiltrated? The black sun shook with laughter. *Ahem. My gaze falls upon them at various, rigid intervals—certain phases of the moon, solar conjunctions, et cetera. Keyholes open between the material realms and the Great Dark and a brief exchange can occur. A dry hump, in human terms.*

X's for Eyes

Mac glanced at the crystal lodged in his gut. He realized it somehow reflected in the evil gaze of the following pack—it pulsed and so did their many sets of eyes. "In the interest of saving ourselves some pain, let me lay it on the table. I won't help revive you."

Fear not. My revivification cannot be completed by mortal rituals or mortal bloodshed. Perhaps the stars themselves can affect my ascendance. Your own sun will have dwindled to a cinder.

"Be that as it may, the cultists seem quite sure of their mission."

Tom is a bit of a false prophet. His favorite trick is to twist weak minds, to convince them he's a herald for my numinous majesty rather than an exiled brat. These men wish to establish greater communion. Tom suggests I might be restored to full glory with the proper rituals and concomitant astronomical alignment. A damned lie, alas. Silly bastards will do anything to win favor with the unholiest of the unholy.

"What's the point in misleading his own followers? I don't get the impression he cares for material wealth. He's no evangelist."

Make no mistake, certain favored mortals know the truth and consider Tom and his servitors an enemy for my affection. As to why he mistreats his own followers so shabbily? Base lust, sad to say. Tom eats some and rapes the sanity from others. Their pitiful appeals to greater meaning delight him. Isn't that the way of your kind, though? To attribute motives and pattern to the inscrutable and the ineffable?

"He implanted a post hypnotic suggestion in my mind that permitted me to open the way."

Indeed, Tom sent you to me. He has an agenda.

"I wonder what that could be."

His motive will become apparent. In the meantime, trust that I personally hold no malice for the people of the Earth. A teeny-tiny piece of me that sheared off during the trilobite era of your world's prehistory can be malicious. My lesser self remains fast asleep and harmless for eternity—unless some idiot rouses it.

"Swell," Mac shook his head. "Sheared off when you tried to invade? What happened? Too much god to squeeze through the portal? Took it out on Tom when the door snapped shut? Pardon me if I withhold my trust regarding your intentions."

Oh, come now. Bygones should be bygones after a few hundred million years. Ruling over invertebrates did not excite me. I withdrew.

My circumstances changed. You might say I went through a rough patch. Here we are.

"We're here because NCY-93 flew off course and fell into your clutches . . . "

There are no accidents. Think clearly. Think as a Tooms older than nine.

"Oh. I'm an idiot." Mac smiled bitterly. "The trip to photograph Pluto was a ruse. The malfunction of the drive also a ruse. The Great Dark was always the destination." He understood with horrifying certainty that Granddad and Dad were fully aware of Mr. Gray. They'd designed a probe to travel into a parallel universe and gather unholy knowledge from a source of incalculable evil. He could imagine their smug grins as they anticipated the launch, and their resultant fury when the probe blew apart before escaping the Earth's gravity. Which held true? The reality wherein Nancy crashed with a dire payload, or the reality wherein the probe exploded?

Ask me no questions and I'll tell you no lies. This you may have for free—whatever you suppose, you are only half right. However deep you think the rabbit hole descends, it goes deeper. The ground vibrated and cracked. In the near distance, a metal ziggurat rose from the dust. The structure appeared identical to the one frozen inside the Ugruk Glacier. A doorway spiraled open.

This planet and its inhabitants slaked my desires in happier times. An advanced species lies buried beneath these wastes. I annihilated the last of them centuries ago. Their doors remain. Their projectors.

"Your son designed this one as well, I suppose."

No, my daughter did. Hell of an inventor, that girl. Step through the membrane from this reality and be reunited with Drederick. Fix him in your mind. The cogs of the universe will slip and align.

"Yes, and after the hugs and teary kisses?"

Arthur Navarro is not lost to you. The Arthur who returned to your world was a candle flicker of himself. The best of his life force resides in the outermost reaches of my honeycomb prison.

"Fine news, sir. Tell me the catch."

The catch is you and your devious kin will continue to dance for my amusement. Drederick is near the Lagerstätte, my web of death dreams. Go to him, together you'll retrieve your friend and all will be well. Or you'll die horribly. It's always a tossup.

X's for Eyes

"I'd dance a jig to see Arthur returned to the living. On the other hoof, this sure as heck sounds like a deal with the devil."

Naturally it is, you little shit. I advise you to run.

The pack of shadows closed rapidly. These were not wolves. Each figure crawling in the dust was a contorted and ravening doppelganger of Mac himself. Some were wizened babies. Others were infantile ancients. All of them were starved. He ran.

The Night Jungle

Arthur whispered, *This way. This way.*

Dred stepped through an infinity of dead stars. He opened his eyes and a night jungle stretched endlessly. The transition from arctic to tropical was dramatic. Ripe tropical heat smothered and leeched the boys' strength. Tiny stinging flies swarmed from the reeds and crawled into their eyes and noses and feasted upon their sweat. Birds chattered. Great beasts coughed and growled in the undergrowth.

Physics behaved strangely here—gravity pulled more strongly; Crabbe remarked it felt as if he slogged in boots filled with lead. A fishbowl effect created the illusion that everything, including their own bodies, elongated slightly. Around them, the shrouded landscape bent as if in the throes of a violent, soundless storm. It required some adjustment on the boys' part.

And what of Macbeth? Neither of them had mentioned Mac or his conspicuous absence. They'd emerged from the maze and called for him until their throats were raw. Soon after, screams had pealed from the jungle depths and discovering their source became the priority mission. Each scream flickered white as a lightning whipcrack against the underside of the black dome sky. Some emanated near at hand; others echoed far away. Dred and Crabbe stumbled in pursuit downstream along the dirt bank of a river. The flashes of light illuminated an impenetrable jungle inland and more of the same on the opposite bank.

Whenever the lightning flared at a perfect angle, Dred glimpsed objects trapped in the sticky black sky—a deep space probe trailing frozen sparks; planets and asteroids, also snared and motionless; Mother in ceremonial raiment, great wings unfurled; and the snarling visages of Granddad, Dad, and Uncle Andronicus, enmeshed in the cosmic spider web.

Dred and Crabbe crept along the river for hours or days. Impossible to tell with neither sun nor stars to guide them through darkness. The horizon, when it revealed itself, was outlined in seething crimson that brightened and ebbed. They marked the passage of time by the cycles of thirst, hunger, and exhaustion. Thirst was slaked at infrequent springs. Hunger was sated by a satchel of dates, jerky, and nuts Crabbe had tucked into his belt along with flint and tinder. Sleep proved most difficult and the boys did so in shifts lest some predator sneak upon them.

A long while passed before Dred recognized the tormented cries. He stifled a sob of his own. Emotional weakness was hazardous to one's health in the Tooms family. "It's Arthur," he said to Crabbe.

"Yeah, I was afraid to admit it. What does it mean? I read about his funeral in the paper. Navarro is stone dead, right?"

"As three-o'clock." Dred didn't say he'd thought until that very moment the screams were Mac's and his emotion was acute relief. "Am I dreaming? Trapped inside my headset? I doubt my luck is that good. Could this be a land of eternal darkness? The River Styx leadin' us toward Pluto himself?"

"Ain't there supposed to be a boatman? Angels? I don't see any."

Dred shrugged. "There are loads of realities, one layered upon another. Frequencies. We might've landed in some ultimate future or on a planet orbitin' a star so far beyond the rim of the universe physical law is trumped." His Dreamtime programming was occasionally supplemented with lectures from Sword scientists. Doctors Navarro and Souza loved to hold forth regarding parallel dimensions, time paradoxes, astral projection, and quantum entanglement; to which Dred listened with half an ear. At the moment he regretted his years of insouciance.

The pair rested next to a stream that flowed through tall grass and merged with the river. Such was their thirst they risked scooping handfuls of the warm, brackish water into their mouths.

"*I'll* be gone to hell if this ain't swimmin' with brain parasites," Crabbe said, his face an off kilter smudge in the near darkness. He slurped another mouthful and wiped his hand on his shirt. It left a dark smear. "Thick as pea soup up there. Surely no jungle could flourish without sunlight."

"The wilderness feeds upon death," Dred said, quoting Sifu Kung Fan. Another scream rolled across the land and the canopy rustled with disquieted animals. The obsidian sky reflected an anguished phantom visage that stretched and dissipated within moments.

Crabbe spat. "My great granddad survived a shipwreck on the South Seas. He lived alone for three years on an island you could piss across. Two uncles disappeared into the Amazon and came out again the wiser after nine months. Another got lost in the Yukon Territory and hiked three hundred miles to civilization. A whole slew of my kin served in both world wars and had planes and boats shot out from under 'em. Every man jack swam, or walked, or crawled his way back to the world. It would dishonor Crabbe tradition to not walk out of this predicament."

"Heck, I'll count my lucky stars you're along. Otherwise I'd surely have curled into a ball and waited for the end." Dred slapped his friend on the back to show his words were in jest, mainly.

Tigers stalked the jungle. A formidable specimen, twelve feet end to end, and striped white and black, paced the boys for several miles, until it finally vanished into the velvet undergrowth. Crabbe fashioned spears from fallen branches and risked a campfire to harden the pointy ends.

On what might have been the fourth day of their journey, echoes of a terrible clamor drifted to them around a river bend—a guttural chorus of whoops rose and fell in discordant rhythm with shrill blatts of flutes and the omnipresent din of Arthur's shrieks. The boys stooped to conceal themselves among the bushes. Soon they beheld an encampment across the water. Several naked giantesses danced around a bonfire that blazed pure white as molten gold and sent forth a plume of white smoke.

The giantesses loomed as tall as any three mortal women standing upon one another's shoulders. Perhaps they'd survived a recent battle, for bruises and lacerations marked them and they drank heavily from a communal gourd. Lushly compelling as their bodies might be, less attractive, to Dred's thinking, were their gargoyle heads and cyclops eyes that glinted with fearful malice in the leaping flames. Their hair coiled in tall beehives. Apparently the giantesses resided elsewhere for no dwelling structure was evident; only poles driven into the trampled earth, each surmounted by the bloodied skull of some hapless beast or humanoid. The boys exchanged glances of awe and fear and then quietly moved away.

They did not get far.

"Hail, trespassers. I am Noman, collector of lost dreamers." A cyclops stepped from the brush and blocked the path. She dressed in a leather harness. Light from the bonfire sparked in her buckles and along the edge of a bronze sword in her hand. The pupil of her baleful eye bubbled and retracted from the fire glare. "This is the sacred river, Alph. It flows from a cleft in the mountains, the womb of Gaia herself. Her virgin claret stains your lips, your teeth. Foolish children. Come with me to the fire. You will die out here."

"You've seen . . . It," Dred said. "You've seen the Red Sultan."

"So shall you."

"The screaming," Crabbe said.

"Frightened?" Her reply might've been for either of them. She chuckled. "The shrieks of an immortal titan stuck fast in the web of the Underworld. He gave us fire. Eons past. His very name is forgotten. The God Heads were displeased. So the titan suffers." She leaned forward to Dred's level. "Come with me, children. The Underworld lies near and it is ever hungry."

"Thanks for the advice," Crabbe said, and leaped forward and plunged his spear into her widening eye until the point burst through the opposite side in a splash of bone and brain. The cyclops sank to her knees and toppled sideways. She lay twitching in a thickening pool of blood. Her beehive hair spilled in glorious waves upon the dirt.

"She might've been friendly," Dred said, although he doubted it.

Crabbe pointed to a lumpy shadow swinging among branches near head-height. Dred poked it with his spear until it swayed into a beam of firelight—small arms and legs distended from a net. Small eyes blinked and small mouths worked in mute horror. Other child faces were slack or made death grimaces. Some wore nightcaps and pajamas. He prodded again with his spear butt and the whole squirming mass revolved into darkness again.

The boys looted the cyclops' corpse of a waterskin and various sundries and hurried onward. The jungle thinned and gave way to a plain. The river curved into abiding gloom. However, Arthur's phantom shrieks grew more intense, rebounding from a line of shadowy peaks; specifically a volcano that would not have seemed amiss in a Saturday matinee adventure program.

They climbed through foothills and boulder fields, then along a dry creek bed that deepened into a ravine where ancient lava flowed. The ravine gouged its way into a canyon and darkness fell upon them. Dred fashioned torches from bundles of twigs and strips of his shirt. Crabbe dipped the torches in pitch from the cyclops' supplies and ignited one and they proceeded upward, cocooned in a reddish bell of light. In time, the pair emerged on a slope near the rim of the volcano.

Battered and exhausted, the boys made the summit.

Dred regarded the caldera and what awaited them therein. "Aw, no." Tears of horror spilled over his cheeks.

At the Caldera of the Mountain of Hell

My slaves will *serve you well*, the black sun said as Mac bolted into the ziggurat. The alien god then whispered a profane and awful string of syllables. Mac instantly forgot, but he detected it lurking like an infestation of maggots within a pocket of his brain. *Ironic that the barb of my name fits so snugly in the divot Tom dug in your subconscious. Utter the curse and you will find succor.*

Mac traveled at improbable velocity through freezing nothingness. Wheedles of an idiot flute trailed his passage. He materialized on the rim of a caldera in a night land. "Bloody hell," he said.

"In this perversion of reality, our manifestation is largely symbolic," Great-great-great grandfather Seneca Tooms said in a voice of thunder. His disembodied head gently revolved, tethered by a cord of nerve fiber that descended from an iris in a black dome of sky. He floated alongside seven other long-deceased Tooms patriarchs—terrifying busts (an anti-Rushmore) hewn from the necks of high-rise colossuses to form a ghastly mobile of Olympian proportions. Ichor dripped from the iris along the exposed nerve cords and spattered their leering visages. Fat drops beaded on their lashes and hung from their noses. Below lay the throat of the caldera, oozing dank mists.

"Largely, not utterly," Great-grandfather Atticus said. His tongue distended and retracted with a will of its own.

"We guard the way," Great Uncle Cotton Tooms said. "We lick clean the unwashed. We devour the unwary. We vomit the unworthy."

"We'd shit em," Atticus said. "But there's not an asshole between the eight of us."

None of the others spoke. Mordechai, Theocles, and Zane glared and smacked their squirming lips. Solomon and Hewitt gaped in inchoate rage or exultation. Their protuberant eyes shifted in constellations of congealed blood and shattered veins. The idiot flute melody issued from their slack mouths.

The mists of the caldera receded and a panoply of shivering star fields was revealed. Arthur Navarro, grown to titanic dimensions, lay spread eagle upon a tor of black crystal jutting from the ocean of galaxies. His limbs were skewered with crystal spikes. Suppurating wounds masked him. Grisly lacerations crisscrossed his immense form. A vulture-headed woman clad in a shimmering white girdle crouched atop his chest. She dipped her beak into his exposed intestines. Titan-Arthur howled and the stars rippled and changed.

Dred and Telemachus Crabbe straggled at that very moment over the rim of the volcano. "Mother!" Dred fell to his knees with all the drama of an actor in a production of Shakespeare. Vulture-headed goddess or not, a mama's boy always recognizes his own mother.

"I'm having an epiphany about our lineage," Mac said. He shuffled his feet. His toes poked through the ragged mukluks. "Toomses are all the evil of the world. Aren't we?"

"Most of it for the last millennium, for damn sure!" Atticus cackled and his eyes slipped in their cavernous sockets.

Mac recalled Grandfather Danzig's love of models—planes, ships, cities. Especially cities. He could imagine the old man moving pieces on a board, arranging assassinations, kidnappings, rocket launches, and remote expeditions, all with the ultimate goal of manipulating his grandsons into fight or flight responses. "Why the charade of the probe? The insanity with poor Arthur and his brothers? Why fake an expedition to unearth the ziggurat? If the Tooms patriarchs are allied with Mr. Gray, the Emperor, whatever you call it, then they know everything. They set the cult upon us. Allowed Zircon to kidnap us. Risked our lives with the corrupted Spetsnaz and the maze . . . Why? Is this some bizarre test? A trial?"

"Gauntlet," Dred said, still clutching his head in both hands as he rocked. "Mac, it's a gauntlet."

"Gauntlet!" the heads cried in unison and the earth trembled and small rock slides plunged into outer space.

"The Gauntlet is an ancient family rite," Seneca said. "On every world and across infinite realities, different families, but always the same gods and the same rite. Resources, peons, the lives of your friends, your less gifted relatives . . . expendable in the pursuit of true power. It's a rare son of the old blood who runs the Gauntlet. Lear and Andronicus were favored to make a run—Mervin, Nestor, and Gage were not. Only the Toomses who undertake and survive this harrowing are fit to enter the inner circle. Congratulations, kids!"

Mac said, "Our bothers . . . They died in the Gauntlet?"

Seneca laughed. "No, silly boy. Your uncle slaughtered them. He's a firebrand, our dear Andronicus."

"Didn't stand before us with knocking knees or pissed pants, either," Cotton said.

"Are you afraid to gaze upon the unholy radiance of our patron in darkness?" Atticus rolled his gaze upward to indicate the seeping vault. "Shall I open the way? Shall I send you before our benefactor?"

Dred wailed and covered his face. Mac took a protective step toward his brother.

"Oh, calm yourselves. In the fullness of time, you *may* become one of us, an eternal servant of the Gray Eminence. Meanwhile, the worlds are your oysters. Shuck them and make merry."

"How now?" Crabbe said. He stood, pale and blank, as if perceiving his surroundings as a violent hallucination.

"Be still, cur," Cotton said. "You exist to serve as a dog fetches conies and licks the boots of its master."

Seneca said, "Hold fast, brothers. Far too much golden about this one. I say we corrupt him a tad. Let the aptly named Telemachus partake of the sweetbreads of immortality."

Mac waited for the harrumphs and mutters to subside. "We came to retrieve our friend." He nodded toward Arthur. "If such a thing is possible."

"As you wish, it will be so," Atticus said. "Mortals exist in our domain as consciousness lent substance. Dreams given the illusion of flesh—your corporeal bodies were destroyed instantly within the ziggurat. From minute particles shall you be restored. "

"There *is* a price." Seneca whistled, shrill as a nail through the ear. "Endless suffering."

Theoris Tooms' spine contorted and split in a long vertical slash. A pair of wings unfurled and she shot from her perch upon titan-Arthur. She divided into three smaller, human-sized versions of her principal self. The trio ascended to the rim of the caldera with such speed, Mac was unable to avoid grasping talons that sank into his shoulders and pinned him flat to the dirt. He cried out in agony and she vomited her gory repast down his throat. It went likewise with Dred and Crabbe.

Shock and revulsion overcame Mac. He didn't resist as his mother the vulture goddess bore him on high with two powerful beats of her wings. She flung him into the gaping maw of Atticus. Great-great-great Granddad champed his teeth on Mac's thrashing body and ground his bones to meal.

Placental Expulsion

Mid-August of 1956, The *Anchorage Daily News* reported that a beluga whale beached herself near the port of Whittier, Alaska. The cow whale had been dead several days and was a feast for carrion birds when a kayaker spotted her. The man approached the carcass and prodded it with a paddle. He was surprised that the edge of the paddle sank into deliquescing blubber. Gasses of decomposition reacted and the whale burst like a four thousand pound piñata, nearly drowning the fellow.

The paper omitted the rest of the story: four adolescent males were discovered within the remains—curled into the fetal position and comatose. Representatives of Sword Enterprises arrived at the hospital to whisk the mysterious patients away.

Subsequently, the reporter fell into a sizable inheritance and promptly quit journalism. The kayaker vanished while paddling in the sound and is presumed dead.

Tom Foolery

Three weeks at a private sanitarium in upstate New York wasn't all bad if one happened to be a Tooms, or in Telemachus Crabbe's case, a boon companion. Mac and Dred soon recovered sufficiently to swim in the pool, play squash, and devour three four star meals a day. Afternoons were for long strolls around the expansive property, birdwatching, and checking the fences for weak spots. Crabbe did not accompany them on these excursions—he'd lapsed into a state of melancholy. Sequestered in his chamber, Crabbe penned an extensive journal he referred to as preamble to his memoirs. The brothers tactfully avoided mentioning that Mr. Nail would likely confiscate any physical record of the events surrounding Ugruk Glacier.

Scant news penetrated the high walls and electrified fences of the sanitarium. News stories were concocted to explain various odd events; Uncle Nestor and Dr. Bravery apparently emerged from the depths of the glacier unscathed. Numerous Sword operatives and consultants were less fortunate. Scores of men perished in some kind of mining explosion. Page three fodder.

The brothers agreed to dispense with psychiatric modalities and comforting explanations for their night terrors, and day terrors. They clasped hands and swore to remember what happened within the ziggurat and after. They vowed not to dismiss the horrors of the astral beyond as mere hallucinations or temporary mental aberrations. Psychiatrists and Sword propagandists be damned. Neither parent nor uncle nor aunt had deigned to visit them in this wellness prison, so their relatives could be damned too.

Mental trauma notwithstanding, the boys *had* recovered physically; perhaps too well. The old scar on Dred's knee healed without a trace. All of his scars (and Mountain Leopard Temple bestowed many) were gone. The chunk of NCY-93's recording crystal lodged in Mac's gut had melted away. His skin was smooth and unblemished as the day he'd first entered the world. It bothered him to feel almost preternaturally healthy, as if the spring in his step could lead to an effortless leap over the sanitarium wall, or kicking right through it.

One afternoon, they went for their customary ambit of the grounds.

"You, me, Crabbe . . . " Dred tossed a bread crust for the pigeons that clustered around the flagstone walk. "Sword propaganda can deal with the mysteries surrounding us. Arthur was *dead*. Doornail dead. Doesn't it defy the laws of nature for him to exist?"

"Presumed dead," Mac said. The hospital lay far behind them. The path curved along the edge of a real forest that extended up into the Catskills. "Laws of physics, causality, have been satisfied. Besides us, no one ever saw an actual body. We don't count due to special circumstances. Therefore, it is possible he never died. If he never died, from a quantum perspective it isn't important where Arthur was for those months the world thought him extinct. Now he's back with his loving family. Amnesiac, bedridden, emotionally fraught, but alive. Ultimately, that's what counts. Arthur is alive."

"His bothers aren't. Hera drove Hercules mad and he killed his family. Afterward, he dwelt in mortal agony until his betrayal and murder. Will it be the same with Arthur? Will he wander the earth seeking redemption?"

Neither boy mentioned a dream they'd shared between semi-consciousness within the womb of the whale and snapping awake in the hospital. In the beginning, there were three human boys nestled together inside that whale—Mac, Dred, and Crabbe. Arthur had emerged *from them* and separated unto his own fully-formed entity. Regarding the details of this particular matter, perhaps the less said the better.

"And what about Big Black?" Dred said. "Gotta figure it's corrupted, right?"

"I'm operating on the assumption our family and everything we touch corrupted at every level. Big Black is touched by evil, no mistake."

"Cheery."

They walked on, dressed in hospital linen and slippers; a pair of children or little old men preoccupied with the woes of the world.

"The doctors will spring us sooner or later," Dred said.

"Granddad or Dad will okay the papers, sure."

"This has been a nice break. What happens next might not be as pleasant. Frying pan, fire."

Mac shrugged. "A Star Chamber hearing doesn't seem particularly frightening at this point in my career."

"Nah, life ain't bad. We've our health, our looks, and loads of money. Could be worse things than belonging to a family whose patron is an alien god . . . "

"Could there be?"

"Hey, I doubt the subject comes up every day. It's probably like mass—you go on Easter."

The boys exchanged smiles and an uneasy chuckle. An orderly in white approached them, cutting across the slavishly manicured sward. He didn't seem to be in haste, yet closed the distance swiftly. He whistled a soft, repellent tune.

"Hello, Tom." Mac stepped forward to shield his brother.

"*Tom* is it? No more Mr. Mandibole? My, my, how quickly they grow up these days." Tom stopped short and gave a half bow with the grace of a medieval troubadour.

"I recognize ya from somewhere, pal," Dred said. "Drivin' a giant bulldozer . . . ? Weren't ya dead?"

Tom Mandibole brushed imaginary lint from the breast of his ill-fitting uniform. Stitched letters on his breast pocket spelled J.R. LEGRASSE. Traces of blood spackled the cuffs. "Chauffeur, pilot, health inspector, slaughterhouse exsanguinator, nursery attendant, and whorehouse piano player. I am a man of many hats."

"Ya ain't wearing one now," Dred said with a sarcastic smile.

"Ah, I shall rectify. Your gape-mouthed head will serve nicely as a bonnet." Tom's smile was *not* sarcastic in the least.

Mac nodded. "Full circle. You enabled our journey to fulfill a purpose. What *is* your agenda, Tom?"

"Agenda . . . You've been talking to the Roller of Big Cigars. Well, my agenda is the same as it ever was. Picture the way a powdered *whale* of a high society dame will gulp her weight in prawns. *My* weakness is the life essence of primates who take a swim in the Great Dark and return, brimming with eldritch vitality."

"Our rosy cheeks are indeed irresistible," Mac said, casually reaching for a knife that wasn't in his pocket.

"In short, I will knock your heads together and eat you alive, dripping cocktail sauce."

"That was the plan all along," Mac said. "To devour us."

X's for Eyes

"*Allll* along. My . . . master promises and promises, yet seldom delivers. I have determined to make my own fun from here on." Tom cracked his knuckles and yawned, very wide. "Scream, struggle, run . . . I care not." He spread his arms for a hug. His midsection punched inward simultaneous with a rifle boom behind the boys. He flew backward and lay supine, inert. Small flames nibbled fabric around the charred hole in his chest.

Mr. Kowalski hobbled from the bushes. He worked to reload a double barreled elephant gun. The man wore a nondescript gray suit and homburg. His face and hands were heavily bruised and pink with sutured cuts. He sucked air through his teeth in the manner of one who's suffered grievous injuries. Getting stabbed by a platoon of Spetsnaz couldn't be salubrious. "Best to get behind me, lads. Tom won't go quietly."

"Mr. Shrike, we are in your debt," Mac said as the puzzle pieces snapped into place. He recalled how the man had shrugged off death blows to wreak havoc among the Russian mercenaries at the glacier. The bland "Mr. Kowalski" and his vague job attachment to the expedition had proven the perfect cover for the legendary assassin.

"Hardly. Your grandfather paid through the nose for me to be a watchdog. I see why he didn't haggle over my retainer. The old bastard."

Tom sat up like a switchblade snapping open. The hole in his chest coagulated and began to knit. "Holland and Holland 500 Nitro, unless I miss my guess. Damn bracing!" He regarded Mr. Shrike. "Dear man, fire that weapon again and I'm going to shove it as far up your—"

"Brother, cover your ears. Excuse me, Tom?" Mac pursed his lips. The maggoty scribbles the black sun had whispered into his subconscious aligned, lethal as a spearhead.

In the instant before it started, Dred slapped Mr. Shrike's gun aside and said, "Trust me!" He hunkered and covered his ears. The man emulated him.

Mac emitted a piercing whistle. The blast went on for no more than three seconds and no less than an eternity.

Tom Mandibole's smile slithered away. He shuddered. His arms thrust upward, jittering in Pentecostal fervor. He pirouetted to invisible music that carried him off toward a wall strewn with creepers. Tom climbed the wall with three convulsive gestures and teetered atop it, eyes streaming black tears. He performed a backward somersault and was gone.

Mac collapsed to one knee. His senses swung on a pendulum to and from an abyss. He gagged until a handful of fragmented black crystals pattered into the grass. These he covered with a swipe of dirt and twigs. Slightly recovered, he stood and attempted nonchalance. His skull felt warped as taffy on a hot day.

"Mac, are ya okay?" Dred scrutinized him intently.

"Right as rain, brother." It had taken Mac considerable effort to recall the proper idiom.

Mr. Shrike shook his head as a klaxon began winding from the hospital proper. "Whole institution will be on the way in a minute. You lads want to come with? I've a rope ladder on a section of the wall, just past the woods . . . "

Mac waved him off. "Thanks anyway. We'll go take our medicine." After Mr. Shrike had departed, the brothers walked toward the buildings where staff gathered. The siren continued to blare.

"Sure we shouldn't have gone with him?" Dred said. "Laid low a while? That Tom Mandibole fellow might double back for another go at us . . . "

"What, and miss my four o'clock sponge bath from Nurse Carruthers? Be serious, kid."

"Good point. Objection withdrawn," Dred said.

The sun slid from behind a low bank of clouds and burned white. Mac half expected it to speak to him, but it didn't.

About the Author

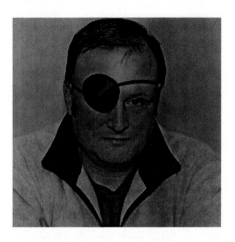

Laird Barron spent his early years in Alaska, where he raced the Iditarod three times during the early 1990s and worked as fisherman on the Bering Sea. He is the author of several books, including The Croning, The Imago Sequence, Occultation, The Light Is the Darkness, and The Beautiful Thing That Awaits Us All. His work has also appeared in many magazines and anthologies. An expatriate Alaskan, Barron currently resides in upstate New York.

Boiled Americans by Matthew Allen Rose

Boiled Americans is a puzzle box in book form, inspired by the violence of living in urban America and exploding the tendency to forget or ignore.

Great American Slasher by David C. Hayes

Baseball, apple pie . . . and murder.

The Bohemian Guide to Monogamy
by Andrew Armacost

Here, a strange labyrinth of interlinked short fiction assembles itself into a darkly moving novella that deftly explores the bottomless pain and pleasure of love and commitment, the hinterland between youth and adulthood.

Surreal Worlds edited by Sean Leonard

An anthology of surrealistic compositions created by some of the finest names in genre fiction. A showcase of international talent undaunted by the conventions of language and common narrative structures. Here is timelessness. Here is Surreal Worlds

How to Succesfully Kidnap Strangers by Max Booth III

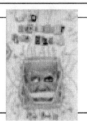

Do not respond to bad reviews. If you must respond to bad reviews, please do not kidnap the reviewer.

ADHD Vampire by Matthew Vaughn

He came, he conquered, he was distracted a lot

Notes from the Guts of a Hippo
by Grant Wamack

A rugged journalist travels to Brazil in search of a missing hippo researcher and the notes left behind lead to something earth shatteringly revelatory.

All Art is Junk by R. A. Harris

Lana Rivers, a girl with paintbrush hair, is missing and it's up to Lancelot, her cyborg knight, and his bionic conjoined twin, Cilia, to find her before her evil father, a disrespected artist turned mad-scientist, performs a terrible experiment on her.

Cherub by David C. Hayes

Cherub wasn't like the other boys—too slow, too rough—but he didn't deserve what that hospital did to him, and now he will make them pay.

Skinners by Adam Millard

Los Angeles, the City of Angels. At least, that's what the brochure says. What it fails to mention is the earthquakes. Oh, and the flesh-eating creatures lying dormant beneath the concrete, waiting for the chance to surface once again. Their wait is over . . .

The After-Life Story of Pork Knuckles Malone by MP Johnson

What's a farm boy to do when his pet pig becomes an evil, decaying hunk of ham with slime-spewing psychic powers?

A Lightbulb's Lament by Grant Wamack

A gentleman with a lightbulb for head wakes up in a world full of darkness, hooks up with a beautiful ex-prostitute, and an old man who can heal people; he travels down south to find the mysterious Creator.

The Horror Show by Vincenzo Bilof

A poetry novel—a narcoleptic, amnesiac Nobel Prize-winning poet becomes the subject of an experiment to cure madness.

Beyond by Jordan Krall

From Jerusalem to Mars, psychiatry and the unraveling of the universe

Gravity Comics Massacre
by Vincenzo Bilof

An absolutely shitty novella involving comic books, aliens, a serial killer, teenagers in an abandoned town, horror-trope dream sequences, and an ending you're going to hate.

Glue by Scott Lange

Sticky bowels and sticky situations.

Ascent by Matthew Bialer

Is the 8 foot tall creature haunting a small town in Iowa in the fall of the year 1903 the product of a hoax and collective imagination or was it one of the first documented paranormal event in America? This epic poem grapples with these questions.

Fecal Terror by David Bernstein

A killer turd is on the loose!

The Fairy Princess of Trains
by Christopher Boyle

Danny's mediocre life turns upside-down when his couch starts whispering to him. Then he's charged with a supernatural mission: Rescue the Fairy Princess of Trains.

Terence, Mephisto & Viscera Eyes
by Chris Kelso

9 new science fiction stories from Chris Kelso

Industrial Carpet Drag by Bruce Taylor

Chemicals make you do great things!

Bizarro Bizarro: An Anthology

The finest bizarro short stories from 2013.

Necrosaurus Rex by Nicolas Day

Necrosaurus Rex tells the tale of Martin, a simple janitor, who takes an unfortunate trip through time, becomes a violent mutant, and the father of us all. There's 14 billion years crushed inside these pages, and most of them are pretty nasty.

Day of the Milkman by S. T. Cartledge

In a world dominated by the milk industry, only one milkman survives after a terrible storm sinks all the ships and throws the Great White Sea out of balance.

Moosejaw Frontier by Chris Kelso

An unapologetic disaster of metafiction

The Boy Who Loved Death by Hal Duncan

From blackest humour to bleakest horror, with twisted relish, Hal Duncan's eighteen tales dig into death—and the life that goes with it.

CPSIA information can be obtained
at www.ICGtesting.com
Printed in the USA
FFOW04n2139160116
20452FF